Steven K. Wooden

DIMENSIONS

DIMENSIONS

Steven Wooden

---KLP---
An Imprint of Kent-Fiction and Literary Publishing

DIMENSIONS

Kent-Fiction and Literary Publishing

Cover Photography and Design by Steven Wooden
Copyedits by Deb Hoehn

ISBN-13: 978-0692495896
ISBN-10: 0692495894

For my Parents

Thomas & Helen Wooden

ACKNOWLEDGEMENTS

I could not have completed this book without the support of my loving friends and family.

The Family: Pamela, Thomas, Marcia, Barbara and Anthony. Thank you for your opinions, advice, constructive critiques, business knowledge and ongoing encouragement throughout this process.

The Friends: Le Mons, Passion Czar and long-term friend, for whom no idea is too big and where no abstract thought is lost. You totally get where I'm coming from and I suspect many people are not blessed with a friend like you! E. Ballou, my front line reader and friend whose honesty and critical insight helped me move beyond the early draft stages of my book. Mr. J. Anderson, thank you for your ear and high level concept critiques.

To the cover to cover readers: M. Wooden, P. Mountain, T. Wooden Sr., S. Mountain, B. Gurecki, Le Mons, P. Wooden and Ms. J. Newton. Thanks for your participation in the most difficult and critical part of the process. Feedback from even the smartest readers is not easy, especially when they have a personal relationship with the author. This group delivered! Thank you, thank you. The sequel is coming soon!!!

I'd also like to thank Art & Pauline, A. Mountain and my UMASS Medical School family, for your support and input in constructing my book cover.

Finally, to JT Newton for your love, encouragement and patience while reading hours and hours of chapters out loud. I'm very lucky to have you in my life.

DIMENSIONS

Chapter 1

---The Benign---

One a.m. marked the arrival of another unpredictable New England fall. Change was in the air. It could either be embraced or resisted, but it was inevitable.

Paulis Blunt laid in bed dissolving in and out of sleep, searching for some reason in his young life. In spite of his obvious fatigue, sleep had eluded him. He kept changing positions, trying to find his comfort zone. The sheets were crumpled all the way down to his dusty feet, and a pillow had fallen to the floor as a restless storm moved against the night.

It occurred to him that his parents must have left the television on, because he kept hearing hollow whispers in the distance. The holographic computer monitor faintly glowed, making the colorful collection of box tops on the walls flicker. The water was also running, or maybe it was just the bathroom self-cleaning again. His mind raced from one tangent to the next as his wiry fifteen-year-old frame flinched with uncertainty.

Paulis thought about the early hour he must arise to accomplish the obligations that awaited him. The new school required that his inner cheek be swabbed for DNA, just like they did for that innocent girl now comatose in the hospital. Paulis pondered the girl's fate, and wondered who he must become to do what would be expected. This was the first full day that he hadn't thought about the foreign tissue implanted in his finger, but tonight it throbbed.

Suddenly there was a noise downstairs, though he had trouble isolating the sound over the howling wind. As the wind momentarily subsided the noise could be heard again, but this time, it carefully ascended the stairs. The sound of footsteps kept stopping and starting, until finally, there was a resting creak outside his door.

The night had become darker. All Paulis's heavy eyes could see were the shadows from the swaying trees against the ceiling. The room shifted, and deceptively surged with the dangerous undercurrent that lurked in the background. Paulis felt the uneasy air of someone in the room. His suspicions were confirmed when the dresser drawer shook and quietly slid. Maybe it was his mother, intrusively gnawing at his privacy; her neurotic gift draped in parental concern and obligation.

The sound closed in, and moments later, he felt the presence of someone next to him. A woman's porcelain face came into focus, her steamy breath radiating on his neck from above. His eyes could shift, but it was painful to move them to the extreme. Although Paulis was unable to capture the details of the woman's face, she seemed familiar but unrecognizable. Maybe they met in another life, or perhaps in that realm they say exists between blinks. He saw that she was practically naked. Her sparkling white skin bounced against the night, causing his sex to stir. There were two calculators attached to her breasts, and another suspended from the waist, covering her private place.

While it seemed that Paulis was awake, his legs and arms would not move, and he could barely control his quickened breathing. He tried to rise up, but his neck muscles were tense, and his head was just too heavy. Paulis was drugged with fleeting thoughts of impending doom and wondered why this was happening. It was her again, but this time, she intended to claim his soul.

The intruder hovered above him, holding something that looked like a gun. She smiled and aimed it at him as her blue eyes locked with his. Paulis was captivated by her beauty, but her aggressive posture rattled his innocent notions of love. He couldn't understand why she wanted to hurt him; it didn't seem fair. His mind said run, but he wasn't able to move. He couldn't even scream. The bed had become his prison, or maybe his tomb. Was his crazy life journey about to end before it had begun?

The room was still, and the air was thick with humidity. No one could hear Paulis's silent screams for mercy. She pushed the gun through his lips and slowly moved it around. He salivated, as a cold and dirty metallic sting filled his mouth.

She paused, relishing his perverted paralysis. Then she loomed over him and shoved the handle of the gun forward with the tip of a fingernail. Paulis gagged, his jaw muscles ached; her eyes so impossibly blue.

"Mutant!" she whispered.

Paulis recognized this tone and secretly found comfort in its familiarity. She sighed, and closed her big, domineering eyes. He was silent as his lids rapidly blinked and a tear ran down his cheek. Paulis inhaled and took in the room's feminine aroma. The desire to recoil was lost.

Suddenly, the bathroom door opened with a baritone, decompressed pop, and the dream woman dispersed into the night like a bead of liquid nitrogen.

Paulis rapidly exhaled, feeling like a ton of bricks had been removed from his chest. He tested his limbs for cooperation and peeled his dry tongue from the roof of his mouth. Quickly, he ran to the bathroom. His sweaty feet struggled as they sucked at the cold floor. Dazed, he splashed his face, and gulped down several handfuls of cold water. His throat expanded and pulled the cool fluid home.

The mirror held his ashy face, his loose dreadlocks suspended on either side. The soft, white lights calmed him and the recently cleaned sink still felt warm. His rational mind said it was only a dream, yet his inner peace had been shaken beyond recovery. He wiped his runny nose and popped a tender zit on the right side of his nostril. Paulis threw more water on his face, and then went back to bed. The bed was cool and damp with perspiration, but he climbed back in, anyway.

The constant rumble of the night infused the backdrop of the real world. An insidious world where actualized pain, was greater than anything his imagination could hold. So Paulis wondered what level of his existence should be held as precious. Should it be the fresh scent of the Downy-soft sheets, blossoming at the back of his nose, or the chemicals intertwined to create the illusion?

Paulis sank with a pillow between his legs and another clutched to his chest. Then he squeezed firmly until they conformed. Soft and still, Paulis waited for his blissful slumber.

Chapter 2

Morning had come, and Paulis descended the wooden stairs leading to the living room. Natural light emanated via the walls of glass and solar panels weaved throughout the ceiling. The effect was a raw feeling, especially in the winter, when the trees were bare. It was like a curtain had been drawn and his family was exposed and vulnerable. Paulis always felt like he was being observed in this room, like a lab rat or convict. The room's leather furniture couldn't have been more than a couple of years old and yet it seemed so worn. He certainly never sat on it. It must be the new thing; his mother had always been up on the new things. Paulis made his way to the dining room, adjacent to the kitchen. He smelled bacon!

"Good morning," said Sarah. "Eggs?"

Paulis sluggishly took a seat at the table. He ran his fingers through his damp brown locks, and rubbed his eyes, in an attempt to hide his disheveled state.

"Where is your father?"

He perked up a bit, but then cautiously retreated. "How should I know? I didn't realize he was back."

Sarah smiled proudly. "He got in last night. Why don't you bring him down while I make the eggs?"

Within a flash, Paulis ran back upstairs in search of his father.

Sarah stood alone in her tall, gleaming kitchen, savoring the familiar aroma as she sipped her coffee. She quietly stared out the window, admiring the rainbow of leaves displaying their beauty, before beginning their final jig.

Sarah's complexion was what they used to call high yellow, but one look at her derriere and there was no doubt that she was a sister. No one believed that she was a day over forty until they learned that she had a teenage boy. She couldn't believe it either, because raising a child had been all-consuming. Still, she happily celebrated each milestone.

Then, one day she caught a glimpse of who he might be as a man. Of course, this meant her own youth was no longer on the table, but who needed youth, when you had the regal beauty that Sarah possessed. She was polished, and could maneuver any circle. As a youth she navigated the streets, learned her manners in college, and then never looked back. She married Roree because he adored her. She was stronger than him, so she trusted him. Roree's face held anxious secrets that his eyes promised to share. He trusted her because he knew she would stick with him until the end. Luckily, their love came later.

Still lost in thought, she moved over to the range, adjusting her clingy skirt as it rose to meet her curvy body. Sarah slid her knuckles under her glasses and rubbed her tired morning eyes. Then she lit a fire under the skillet and drizzled in some virgin olive oil. The big black cast-iron surface immediately absorbed the oil. She cracked an egg, picking out the stray shells as she watched it sizzle to life. The egg's crackling pantomime evoked visions of an audience giving a standing ovation for her unyielding dedication. Then with the flick of a wrist, she flipped the egg and it bled, releasing its unequal yolk of contempt.

Paulis entered his parents' bedroom, to find only scattered luggage and a tussled bed. He stood there for a moment, staring at the BOS sticker on the suitcase, and imagined how robust his father's other life must be. Was it possible to be jealous of a suitcase he thought to himself as he headed for the study.

Roree had flown in from San Diego the night before, where he got grilled by a panel of five directors, regarding an upcoming internet initiative. Roree's life had always been by the book. He worked hard and had his Ph.D. by the age of twenty-seven, despite his father's failure to put him through college. He then married his college sweetheart, and began his pursuit for tenure.

The San Diego team requested his presence after one of his students complained to her father that Roree's teachings were "cult-like and out there." It turned out that this parent recognized that while unconventional, his research was cutting edge. The directors felt that his techniques could be beneficial in moving their own project forward.

Roree thought that because they recruited him, the interview was just a formality. So, he flew to San Diego with an air of confidence. Always packing his hatred and his brilliance, as one fed upon the other. Little did he know that his motives would be called into question.

Roree arrived for the interview in his smoky gray suit accentuated with a burgundy pin-dotted tie. His face was dusted with freckles, but his broad six-foot two inch frame projected an intimidating presence. His platinum gray hair and beard were long enough that one questioned his views on authority, yet obsessively manicured to suppress the hippie that he longed to forget. Roree was in it to win it, and he knew the exact line of bullshit to feed the directors. If he understood anything, it was human nature. He also had a way with words and could charm a cat out of its nip.

However, his problem was reality-based. Buried in his subconscious, he knew that the cat didn't fancy him enough to willingly give up its nip. As a result, any gifts received from the cat were unearned, and laced with false pretense. So, he compartmentalized his rewards where they served him best, and chose to feel nothing else.

His wire-framed glasses contained a prescription that was stronger than needed. This enhanced his vision beyond that of the norm. However, he dared not turn that enhanced vision within. What would be the point? After all, his laser focus was on the task at hand. San Diego was proof that his hard work was not in vain. He was finally approaching the recognition he deserved, and the

Blunt name would finally mean something. Future generations would appreciate the sacrifices it took to pry the world from its tired mold. But first he needed a cup of coffee.

Paulis entered the study, where he found his father at the computer, oblivious to his presence. His father appeared to be in flight, with his tie flung across his shoulder and his collar open exposing bits of toilet paper plastered to his neck by dried blood. Paulis tapped his shoulder and Roree jerked, startled.

"Hey, buddy," said Roree, as he swung around in his chair.

Paulis rolled his eyes. He hated being called buddy. "Mom says breakfast is ready."

Roree saved his work, and then followed his son to the breakfast table.

Paulis sat, playing with his eggs as he thought about his restless night, wondering if he should tell his parents. He was worried that they might think he was crazy or worse, stupid. Suddenly, he felt his cell phone vibrate on his hip, but caught his mother's glare in his periphery, and dared not check it at the table.

"I had a dream."

"I thought I heard you moving about last night. Do you remember much?" asked Sarah.

He peered up. “Well, I remember there being this naked woman in my room.”

Sarah froze and Roree smiled inquisitively. “Oh really?” said Roree.

“Well, she was wearing calculators, so I guess technically she wasn’t naked.” His heart raced as he prepared to tell his story, which had begun to sound more and more absurd as it played out in his head.

His father smiled devilishly. “Did the two of you add your common denominators?” His parents laughed and Sarah motioned to him. “So, what happened?”

Paulis paused in silence. He knew it was only a dream, but now his parents were laughing at him like he was some sort of freak. Maybe he was overreacting. He just needed to keep it together he thought to himself. He focused on his plate as he relived the details of his nightmare now reflecting up from his eggs. Just keep it together.

He cleared his throat. “Nevermind, it was just a dream.”

Sarah and Roree watched him intently, trying to gauge his sudden change in mood. Sarah worried when she saw her boy suffering. He had always been sensitive, and as a child, she could instinctively tell if his mood swings were more of anger than hurt. However, as he’d grown older, her predictions of one over the other had become less reliable.

Her face dropped to his. "Honey, you have to try not to be so sensitive and what happened to your face?"

Paulis rolled his eyes, as he looked at his father. "Maybe you should try to be less insensitive."

"If you keep picking at your face it's gonna leave a scar," said Sarah, referencing the red blotch on the side of his nose.

Roree contemplated his son's remarks, wondering when he was going to stop being so dramatic and grow a pair. Sometimes, he wished he could just shake him, and awaken the man hiding behind that curtain of childhood insecurity.

"We're sorry honey," said Sarah.

Suddenly, everyone became aware of their eggs. After an awkward silence, Roree gave him a smiling question of truce. "How's Dimensions treating you?"

Paulis stared at the smooth, buffed surface on his thumb. Then he rubbed his fingers together and shrugged his shoulders. "It's ok."

Roree leaned in. "Is it that bad? I'm sure you're going to dig deep and make it work."

Paulis's voice cracked with surprise. "I'm glad you're so sure. You're not the one who's been yanked away from all his friends!" He closed his eyes and retraced his words, deciding not to regret any of them.

"Honey, I know it may seem difficult now." Sarah searched his eyes, allowing her words to hover a moment, as she clasped his hand. "This is the best place for you to grow."

"Get away from me!" Paulis pulled his hand away. "Nobody bothered to ask what I wanted. You could have asked me what I wanted, before changing my school and ruining my life!"

Roree took a bite of bacon and rubbed his dusty gray beard between his fingers, then his jaw tightened. "Paulis, we're making sacrifices for you to go to this school. I need you to work it out. Do you understand that?"

Paulis dropped his fork on the ceramic plate, watching it jump to life and make more noise than he intended. "What do you think I am, a moron? Why don't you explain it to me?"

Roree gave him a long stare, watching Paulis shift uncomfortably in place. Then he settled down. "They're all smarter than me," admitted Paulis desperately.

"Don't be silly, obviously the school thought you were up for the challenge," said Sarah.

"I'm not silly! They've got everybody's IQ posted on the school website. Everybody knows everything about you before you even open your mouth."

"I know, and is that such a bad thing? If I had known your father's IQ upfront, I would never have married him." She smirked in Roree's direction.

Roree raised a brow at her. "You're not helping. Paulis, you have an opportunity to connect with kids who are interested in learning just like you. You're just as gifted as any of them. I just want you to give it a shot."

Paulis rolled his eyes, trying to stay angry, but was weakened by all the attention. He knew what his parents had gone through to give him every advantage possible. But what if he just wanted some fucking space? He knew there was no chance of that. Certainly there wasn't with the parents he'd been dealt.

Roree continued, "If you still feel this way next year, we'll put you back in with the average kids, so you can go back to being the big fish in that small pond."

He looked his father dead in the eye. "This isn't about needing to feel superior so save the rehearsed psychobabble for your students."

Sarah glared at Roree. "Was that supposed to be helpful?"

"You're not supposed to be pressuring me about this. You could get me in trouble with the school!" Paulis shoved his cup on the table and raced to the kitchen. First Sarah rose to follow him, but Roree stopped her, grabbing her by the arm and then quickly followed behind him to the kitchen.

"Paulis, I'm not pressuring you. I didn't say get straight A's or I'm gonna have your hide! Just give it a chance, that's all I ask." Roree firmly cupped his shoulders. "Come on, I know you can do it."

Paulis felt his abdomen relax, and his chest sink as he turned, staring at his father's strong face. He admired him and hoped he'd grow up to have his confidence and presence. Then he remembered his resentment, and how he was always away or working. He should make more time for him. How smart could he be, if he didn't realize that the greatest gift he could give was free?

Roree beamed at his son. "So let's see that phone they gave you."

"It's just for the students."

Roree extended his hand, smiling. "Give it!"

Paulis pulled his phone from his hip and gave it to his father. Roree grinned as he ran his fingers over the smooth, sleek design. "How do you turn it on?"

Paulis placed his thumb flush with the center groove on the wafer thin black screen, and it exploded to life, with three xylophone tones. The words "*Dimensions Boston*" appeared on the screen. It also displayed Paulis's picture, pulse rate, body temperature and blood pressure. "Wow, this thing is loaded!" said Roree. Then the screen flashed "*unauthorized access*" and faded to black. "I guess it doesn't like me," said Roree.

"Yes, it's quite sophisticated," Paulis snickered under his breath. He took the phone back, and walked past his mother on his way to school.

Sarah waited for Roree to return from the kitchen. "Is he ok?" asked Sarah.

"He's fine. Did you get a chance to proofread my lecture slides?" asked Roree.

"Yes I'm almost done with them. You know your laptop's antivirus was off. You should be careful with that."

"I thought we agreed, you would have them for me today."

Sarah batted her eyes sarcastically. "Roree, I'm so sorry I didn't do all of your work for you on time."

"That's not the point. If you agree to do it, I expect you to finish it, or give me a heads up so I can handle it myself."

"Oh relax, I'm almost done. You know I strained my eyes yesterday, reviewing all those slides. Which reminds me, I'm getting new glasses today before my students' first essays are due."

She gazed at Roree, while draining her mug. "I like the new stuff you added about social class, virtual access and behavior modification driven by user reward systems."

Roree smiled. "Oh, you like that?"

"I'm not sure I buy it, but it's interesting."

"Oh, I forgot; if it's not made of DNA, your brain can't wrap around it." Roree smirked to himself. "So, I guess we should take separate cars today?"

Sarah's face hardened. "Do you think this new school is too much for him?"

"He's being challenged out of his comfort zone, but he'll adapt, and just because he's smart doesn't mean you have to coddle him, like a little porcelain doll. He's gonna thank us for this one day." Roree laughed to himself. "Of course, it's not gonna be today. All we can do is give him opportunities and let that big sponge of his soak them up. Is there any more coffee?"

"I'm not coddling him, and you can get your own damn coffee!" Her voice was overtly controlled and she shook her head in disbelief, though she was not surprised.

Roree had never been a warm father. He thought this was what real men did, and he probably had evidence-based data to support his behavior. But it was the gentle guy, whom nobody else knew, that she fell in love with. She hoped their combined efforts would balance out. After all, a boy needs a strong man in his life.

Roree rose to refill his cup, and Sarah waved her empty mug in his direction. He refilled their cups and rejoined her at the table.

"Oh by the way, Vivian is coming to dinner tonight, so I want you home by 7:00, no excuses."

Roree churned his eyes indignantly and leaned back in his chair until it creaked. Then he sank his teeth into another piece of bacon. "Ok, I'll try."

"Roree, 7:00!"

Chapter 3

Dimensions Boston was founded back in 2016 as a charter school. It was designed to keep Boston at the top of the charts of exceptional preparatory schools in the United States. The external façade of the facility was an unassuming, one-story building. It had beautifully manicured landscapes, with Endless Summer Hydrangeas and stately elm trees, waving behind the towering, gated entrance. Closed circuit surveillance cameras continuously documented the historic events happening at this keen institute of learning.

Upon entering the building, the students stopped at a fingerprint identification station, and then passed through a scanner that checked their bodies for inconsistencies and their electronic devices for viruses. Once on the other side of the scanner, a full-scale stealth bomber suspended from the ceiling, which pointed toward a series of escalators that churned ten stories deep into the earth. The Dimensions cafeteria was situated in the atrium, on the lowest level.

Paulis sat alone in the cafeteria, carefully focused on the chopsticks that maneuvered the sushi to his mouth. He was exhausted from his early morning classes and lack of sleep the night before.

There were several groups of razor blade-thin students having animated discussions, as they swiped at the tables in front of them. There was one girl he recognized from his chemistry class. She had on a brown suede jacket and matching skirt, that made her seem more mature than the rest of her friends.

He took his phone out and placed it on the table, activating it with his thumb in the center. As the phone came to life, it interfaced with the table's electric glass community surface, and opened into a larger interactive touch screen. He swiped through the screens, maneuvering to the GPS chat program. There he saw a cluster of four people approximately twenty feet from him, and a cluster of five approximately thirty feet from him.

"That must be them," he thought to himself. He tapped the cluster of five and saw the names: Isaiah, Kelly, Terry, Pauline and Raymond.

Everybody knew Isaiah; he was sent to Dimensions to save him from himself. Apparently, he was bored one night, so he hacked into the FDA's website and posted the approval of a drug that failed in phase III clinical trials. Had he known the proper protocol, he could have caused a lot of confusion. Attending Dimensions was an attempt to repackage his energy.

Paulis checked the profiles of the girls at Isaiah's table. He tapped Kelly, and her image came up. "Right table, wrong girl." Next he tried Pauline. "Wrong again." He tapped on Terry. "Yes, that's the one!"

He read through her stats:

Academics:
-In good standing, GPA 3.9, IQ 160
Genetic Makeup:
-Genotype expressions- BRCA 1 cancer gene positive, Gay gene positive
-Phenotype expressions- both genes unexpressed
Family:
-Upper middle class, biological parents married

He couldn't believe that she was so smart, and pretty, too. He tapped the bump option and watched her face for a reaction.

A few seconds later, she pulled her phone from her hip, and looked around. The other kids at the table didn't pay any attention to her looking at her phone. She lowered her phone and looked around again. They made eye contact and she smiled to herself. Paulis froze in panic, staring stupidly, wondering what to do next. The girl with the impressive profile had just become real, but he was just an awkward boy with no game plan.

She put her phone away and returned to the group. Paulis smiled and added her to his list of friends.

He couldn't believe what he had just done. He thought maybe he should have waved, because there was absolutely no way he was going to approach her. Of course later she would read his stats, and decide if he was good enough to talk to. Even worse, maybe her parents would tell her not to waste her time with an inferior man who was born missing his two baby toes.

"Oh, fuck it," he thought to himself, at least he wouldn't have to waste time. This time, there was nowhere to hide his insecurities.

Dimensions believed in full disclosure, so the only thing you had to worry about was learning the course material. Social pressures were not centered on facades, or doubts about who knows what. Everything was put on the table, so the truth could never be used against you. You owned and dealt with who you were, so you could focus on your education.

Paulis hated being so exposed, but on some level he was relieved that everybody knew everything. Now he only had to manage other people's reactions as well as his own.

Paulis went back to his lunch, this time choosing his fork over the chopsticks. He looked up every now and then, to see if Terry looked his way. He took another mouthful of sushi, this time with a scoop of the olive-colored stuff from the side of the plate. "Wow!" He'd never understood why his mother was so crazy about it. Rice and raw fish; what's the big deal?

---Home in the Study---

Sarah had spent the afternoon upstairs in the study, which was more like a loft overlooking the living room, encased by a wall of glass. Two large oak tables faced each other, each containing a computer with two linked, twenty-six inch holographic monitors. The surrounding walls were lined with books. She was working on her lecture slides, eyes darting between several open books—*Genetics and Rational Breeding, The Electronics of DNA and Nanotechnology, Eugenics and the Mapping of Natural Selection.*

She gave the same lectures every semester to a new set of students. She could deliver the undergraduate lectures in her sleep, but the graduate students benefitted from a more tailored curriculum. Many of the undergraduate students just stared at her with bewildered looks of defeat. She understood that it was complicated material, and she would have to fail thirty percent of them. She also knew that most of them were just taking the class to fulfill a requirement for graduation, and could care less about where the world was headed.

However, a few of them would fall in love with her and the world of science she unlocked. These students were the ones she returned to reach, year after year. Sarah thought the American students suffered from self-entitlement, and were asleep at the wheel. They still thought that America led the world in technological advancement. On the contrary, it was the foreign students who hungered for her wealth of knowledge, and thus laying the groundwork for a rude awakening. She hoped to change that.

The doorbell rang and Sarah gracefully extended her long, silky legs down the suspended wooden staircase, leading to the front door. She nearly lost her balance as she reached the landing but composed herself, and went for the door. When she opened it she gazed at the impeccably dressed, elderly woman with dark, etched features standing before her.

"Hello mother."

Vivian stared impatiently at her daughter, bundled in her trench coat and then stepped into the living room, welcoming her daughter's embrace. "It's getting chilly out there."

"Yes, it's that time of the year," said Sarah.

As usual, Vivian's eyes immediately surveyed the tall, icy glass room. There were exposed twenty foot beams holding the walls of glass in place. The colorful art reminded her of framed ink blots, designed to evoke some conditioned response. The manner in which the art was evenly placed throughout the room took on a fingerprint of its own. It was unforgiving, and she certainly knew whose idea it was to put this shit up on the walls. Did they really think that people were this derivative?

"Oh Honey, I love your new glasses," said Vivian, as she returned her gaze to her beautiful daughter. "Where are the boys?"

Sarah smiled as she touched the frames on her face. "Thank you! Paulis is studying, and Roree is on his way now."

"Paulis, come down and say hello to Grandma," she yelled.

Vivian looked at Sarah. "Grandma?"

Sarah smiled to herself.

Seconds later, Paulis charged down the stairs, taking them two at a time. "Vivian!" he gave her a breathless hug.

Vivian gave her lanky grandson a quick once-over. "Paulis, you're such a handsome young man. Come and tell me about your new school."

Paulis peeked at his mother. "I need to study until dinner is ready?"

"You can finish after dinner," said Vivian dismissively as she led him toward the living room.

Paulis looked to his mother for permission. Sarah took a deep breath, but never looked his way. Paulis gave his grandmother a quick smile, and then ran back upstairs. He enjoyed studying and he appreciated the discipline it took to achieve greatness, but more importantly, he wasn't interested in discussing how isolated he felt at school with his grandmother.

"Mother, he's got to stick to a strict study schedule," whispered Sarah, as she took Vivian's trench coat and hung it in the closet. She joined her on the sofa.

"You look well, mother. How was Paris?"

"It was tiring. My get up and go is not what it used to be, but I can't complain; I still feel blessed. I brought back several shoeboxes for Paulis." Vivian smiled and settled into her seat. "So, how's your vaccine research coming along?"

Sarah's eyes lit up. "Roree just got in last night from a meeting in San Diego. He may be chosen to join a team that's developing a new internet initiative. I'm helping him compile a database of reliably mapped electronic genomes."

Vivian sighed. "Honey, I meant how's *your* research going?"

Sarah, annoyed, shifted her bottom against the supple leather. "Mother, you've only been here five minutes."

Vivian settled back and slipped off her shoes, once again puzzled by Sarah's willingness to submit her spirit to her husband. "What time did he get in last night?"

Sarah's eyes locked on her mother. "I don't know, it must have been around 2:30 in the morning. Why? I was already dead to the world."

Vivian knowingly squeezed her eyes and shook her head in resignation.

Sarah took her posture in for a moment. "Mother, would you like some wine?"

"Of course, and something smells delicious." She followed Sarah to the kitchen and balanced herself on the granite countertop watching her pour two glasses of Chardonnay.

Vivian stared off into space. "You know, your father was a God-fearing man and he took good care of us, but I had this feeling that something wasn't right." She turned to Sarah. "You know what I mean? There were always little inconsistencies nibbling at my peace. So I got down on my knees and I prayed to the Lord to fix my man!" She closed her eyes and her nostrils flared as her words formed. "But then the Devil got the best of me and I told your father he had to leave or I was gonna have to cut him up."

Sarah rotated her sturdy gold wedding band. "Mother, Roree is nothing like my father, and what is with this obsession you Detroit women have with cutting people?"

"It's shorthand for those thick Niggers like your father who couldn't understand what burning the bra represented. Now, Roree may not be like your father, but he's a lot like my husband. One of these days you're gonna appreciate the difference."

Sarah took in her comments but contemptuously avoided her stare.

Vivian gracefully picked up her glass of wine and searched for Sarah's eyes. "You and I both know there ain't nothing open in Boston at 2:30 in the morning, except somebody's legs."

Sarah pursed her lips and breathed deeply, her neck locked in a subtle tremor as she watched her mother. She hoped that she would not follow in her footsteps and become a bitter, old woman.

Vivian took a sip from her glass as she turned to leave the kitchen. "Don't worry, I'll behave when your Caucasian man gets here."

Sarah watched her leave the kitchen and wondered how she would ever be able to explain the complicated truth to her, if she couldn't even get past Roree's color.

Chapter 4

---Dinner---

Evening had, arrived and the family was seated at the dining room table eating roasted chicken with gravy, sautéed spinach and quinoa. Roree arrived thirty minutes late, as Sarah predicted he would, so everything was on schedule.

"I got called into the office this morning," said Paulis. "They claimed that someone with different pulse characteristics handled my phone this morning, after I fingerprinted it."

"What? That's silly," said Roree. "Pulse rates change all the time!"

"The pulse had different characteristics than mine. They warned me that I can provide you with any information from the school's website you wanted but that I'm solely responsible for operating the phone." Paulis stared at his father. "They said you already knew that."

Vivian swirled her wine glass and glared at Sarah. "I don't like this school. What are they trying to hide? When you were a little girl, the parents were responsible for their children's education. We knew exactly what was going on! Now they're planting microchips in fingers and God knows what else. It's not natural! How do you know you can trust these people?"

Roree engaged Vivian's eyes. "It's a neurotransplant, not a microchip, and they're not hiding anything from us. We know exactly what's going on. These people are experts in leading gifted children to success. They just don't want the families to interfere with the kids' process."

Vivian focused on Roree as she cocked her head to the side and tucked her gray bob behind her earlobe, exposing her diamond and sapphire earring. "Yes, we mustn't interfere with the process, or else we might have to take some responsibility for what happens."

Roree calmly chose his words. "Research has shown that parents sometimes impose their failed aspirations onto their children." He glanced back and forth between Vivian and Sarah. "This is especially true for middle class children from broken homes. Unknowingly, they ruin the learning experience for their children. Dimensions creates a healthy environment for them to excel despite outside sources that may influence them to the contrary."

"That's ridiculous!" shouted Vivian. "What about respect and the influence of family values? What about the word of God or have you forgotten about that?"

Vivian's voice settled just above a whisper. "Didn't that healthy environment almost kill that young girl last semester? The FBI was involved and it was all over the web! You need to pray every day that the Lord has a hand in making a man out of that boy."

Paulis shifted miserably in his seat.

"No, we haven't forgotten about that. I pray every day for my son and my family. You included," said Sarah.

"My parents prayed every day too," said Roree, staring out into space, "and where did it get them? My mother died at forty-five, and my father is a bitter, old man, living on a fixed income."

"Well, you know what they say," said Vivian. "A fool and his money are lucky enough to meet in the first place. Now your mother and everybody else knows what happens to smokers!" Vivian relaxed, convinced that her point had been made. "But I'm not gonna worry. I know the Lord is in the blessing business."

Roree gazed blankly beyond Vivian's soulless face. If she was considered a woman of God, then he was not interested in meeting the deviant backsliders she spoke of with such disdain. The Lord had failed to make an honest woman out of her, so he supposed her ex-husband didn't stand a chance. His palms spewed sweat, inside his clenched fists, buried under the table. He knew that every time Vivian saw his white face, she felt a pimp slap from her daughter. This used to be a source of satisfaction for him, but he knew it really had nothing to do with him. It was just her racist nature. There was a time when he believed Vivian was a sweet woman who cared for him, no matter his color. He was wrong.

Vivian knew his father had been a successful investment banker until he lost everything to a New England family's startup hedge fund. A couple of young brokers basically took him for a ride. His father was a proud man, but when he lost the ability to provide for his family, he could no longer find his dignity. Roree had watched his father, at the age of forty, slowly slump over into an old man. He had some small successes after that, but his reputation with his clients, and with his only son, never recovered.

Vivian knew this, and she knew what it did to his family. Even worse, he knew that Vivian's crude assessment of his family was correct, and he had no intention of allowing history to repeat itself. Roree had already taken his revenge on the family that swindled his father. However, only he knew how that went down. It was his only satisfaction.

Roree sat back in his chair running his sweaty hand through his beard, rationalizing between Vivian's wine glass and her wrinkled face, making himself dizzy. "So, how's your chicken Mother?"

Vivian swirled her glass, "Mine is a little dry, but it's good."

Sarah briefly looked at Roree, noting how he had once again managed to deflect Vivian's venom from himself, onto her.

Paulis felt his phone vibrate on his hip and inconspicuously slipped it from its holster to take a look. It was a text from Terry. His heart jumped.

Sarah looked up. "Paulis, don't you dare!"

Paulis quickly replaced the phone, with the blinking text message taunting him, back into its holster. His pulse raced, and his head spun. Is Terry interested, he thought to himself? Paulis moved to leave the table.

Roree looked over to him. "Where are you going?"

"To the bathroom."

"Paulis, you heard your mother."

Paulis settled back into his seat, twisting from side to side. He raked his fork through his sautéed spinach, trying to figure out how to get away from the table. "Grandma, my teacher says that having only four toes on each foot is a sign of advanced evolution."

Sarah briefly looked at Paulis, noting how he had now joined his father in pitting Vivian against her. He knew the delicate balancing act she had to perform to teach evolution and still maintain her spiritual faith, rooted in Creationism.

"I would agree that maybe your toes are a product of your genetic makeup but I'm not so sure it makes you advanced," said Vivian.

Sarah looked at her mother, horrified. "Mother, what are you saying?"

"Oh what now you're going to pull out that Ph.D.? Child, please," said Vivian.

Paulis began tensing his eyes, looking down, trying to make himself cry. "So you think I'm a deformed freak? That's what they called me at my old school, a deformed freak! You think that's what God intended?"

Vivian looked at Paulis, a little embarrassed by what she'd said, as she carefully placed her glass on the table. "Sometimes, we have to suffer and learn to rely on our faith before we can become the strong individuals God wants us to be."

Roree looked at Vivian, quietly grinding his teeth together. "Vivian, I think you've said enough, and you've certainly had enough."

Vivian didn't dignify his comment with a response.

"Can I go to the bathroom now?" asked Paulis, with an awkward smile on his face.

"Go ahead. Who are you in such a hurry to text, anyway?" asked Sarah.

Paulis knocked over his water while jumping up from the table. "A friend," he said.

“Clean up that mess first,” said Sarah.

Paulis jetted to the kitchen, came back with a towel, and threw it on the puddle of water. Then he ran upstairs with the phone in his hand.

Roree smiled at Sarah. “I think somebody’s got a girlfriend.”

“Thank God,” said Vivian.

Chapter 5

Roree was at the computer with his head between his hands, designing his website, when the cell phone rang. To his surprise it was 11:50 p.m. This was the first time he had looked up since Sarah left to drop her intoxicated mother off to feed the cats, three hours ago.

"Who could be calling at this hour?" he thought to himself. The caller ID read "*Sarah Blunt.*"

"Hello Honey, where are you?" he answered.

He heard an intake of breath and an unfamiliar voice: "Hello is this Roree Blunt?"

Roree's heart thumped as his mind jumped from one dark scenario to the next. "Yes, who is this?"

"Mr. Blunt, my name is Marta; I'm calling from Menino Central Hospital. What is your relation to Sarah Blunt?"

"She's my wife."

"Mr. Blunt, I'm sorry to inform you that your wife was in an automobile accident tonight."

"What!"

"Mr. Blunt… Mr. Blunt, don't panic. We have Sarah here in the emergency room. We need you to come in and take care of some of the details while we look after her, ok?"

Roree made an effort to control his voice, not to tremor, not to crack. "Is she all right?"

"We've got it all under control, but she needs you to be here, ok?"

"Don't bullshit me, Martha."

"It's Marta."

"Whatever; is she ok?"

"Mr. Blunt, we've got it all under control, but she needs you to be here now." Her voice was calm yet firm.

Confused, and still a little rattled, Roree answered. "Of course, I'll be right there. What hospital is she in?"

"Menino Central."

"Ok, I'll be right there." He closed his eyes and the cell line simultaneously. "All right, pull it together," he thought to himself.

Roree turned back to his computer, saved his work and then stumbled into the chair, stubbing his bare toe as he quickly moved out of the study. "God damn it!" Then he moved down the long corridor, drunk with worry, to their bedroom. He put on his shoes, grabbed a jacket and then ran down the wooden stairs. "Oh, shit!" He stopped, took a deep breath, and then ran back up the stairs to Paulis's room.

Entering Paulis's room was like walking into a different world. Things were positioned in odd places, but somehow, it all made sense. Whenever someone bought shoes, the box covers went to Paulis, and he covered the walls with them. The room was dark, except for the screen saver image of a DNA double helix, spinning from clockwise to counterclockwise on his monitor.

Paulis was lying on his back, with his knee tenting a sheet that was pulled forward, covering his upper lip. Paulis's eyelids were twitching, and his posture had assumed the unfamiliar form of a grown man.

Roree approached his son, wondering what adventure he had been set upon tonight. He gently shook his shoulder, but he didn't respond. He shook him again, and this time Paulis jumped, "No!" He swung his open fist, connecting with his father's face. Roree tried, unsuccessfully, to duck and then grabbed Paulis by the arm. Paulis's face was sweaty. Roree began twisting his arm back, but stopped when Paulis flinched in pain.

"Paulis, are you all right?" Roree resisted the irrational urge to twist his arm further behind his head.

"What are you doing?" asked Paulis, disoriented and breathless.

Roree released his arm. “You ok?”

Paulis took a deep breath. “Yes.”

Roree gently touched Paulis’s arm. “Your mother had a little accident with the car and I thought it would be nice if we both went to pick her up from the ER.”

Paulis was still shaking off sleep. “Is she ok?” He wondered if she had totalled the car that was supposed to be his next year. Then, frightening thoughts penetrated his mind. Did they find her lying in a ditch somewhere, and his father was withholding the truth? He tried to control his breathing so his father didn’t think he was overreacting.

“We need to leave now. Get dressed.”

He held his breath, frightened by the nervous tone of his father’s voice. “Ok, I’ll be down in a minute.”

Roree left his son to get ready, still feeling the sting on his cheek. He remembered to grab his wallet and keys before heading back downstairs. Five minutes later, Paulis joined him at the bottom of the stairs.

The twenty minute ride to the hospital seemed like an eternity. Steely Dan’s “Aja” was streaming from Pandora. Roree loved Steely Dan because of the unique lyrics. Once you understood them, the music took it to a different level.

Storrow Drive was hauntingly quiet. Fog crawled through the air as Roree searched the roadsides for evidence of an accident, or any hint that could prepare him for what awaited him at the hospital. From time to time, Roree reached over and reassuringly rubbed Paulis behind the neck, but neither of them uttered a word.

---The ER---

"Hello, I'm Dr. Blunt. I'm here for my wife, Sarah Blunt."

"Yes, Dr. Blunt, are you a physician here?"

"No."

The receptionist checked for his wife's name, then gave him an electronic tablet. "Yes, we've been expecting you; have a seat and fill this out. Her physician will be with you shortly." The receptionist motioned for the next person in line to move forward, but Roree blocked the way.

Roree noted that she couldn't have been more than nineteen years old, and her makeup was too heavy. "Can you please tell me what's going on with my wife? She was in a car accident!" Paulis moved up to his father's side when he heard the tension in his voice.

The receptionist stopped chewing her gum and looked inquisitively between Roree and Paulis, admiring his tan mulatto features and his delicate dreadlocks. "No, but someone will be with you soon. Please take a seat." She smiled firmly, resumed her chewing and motioned for the next person to move forward.

Roree and Paulis sat in the midst of what resembled Manhattan rush hour. There was a portly woman with outspoken hair sitting next to them, smelling of mothballs and garlic, grasping at her stomach. Across from them was a man with wide nostrils and bleached teeth. He was holding a bloody towel wrapped around his forearm as he nodded off to sleep. There was a toddler fretting as if his cheeks were stuffed with rattles, rhythmically echoing off his mother's fluffy bosom.

The big, hungry security guard propped himself against the wall gently bouncing his billy club against his muscular calf. He assumed control with a muted stare like an anatomical extension of his surroundings. There was a little white-haired lady with wrinkled skin perched in the corner, with a stunned look on her face. Her mouth gaped open, hungrily sucking at the oxygen mask she clutched with her bony fingers. The lady's neck was stilted by two bulging columns of muscle, and her throat was dissecting through her dusty skin.

Roree moved his shoulder against Paulis, attempting to speak like a ventriloquist. "Don't stare."

Paulis looked at his father, and then turned his attention back to the white haired lady. "Why aren't they helping her?"

Roree briefly thought about his mother and her long struggle with lung cancer. His father spent every penny they had making her comfortable, but had psychologically checked out, leaving him to comfort her. "Somebody's going to help her," said Roree.

Paulis scanned the room and then looked at his father. "I'm skeptical."

Roree put his arm around his son. "Don't worry."

Paulis allowed his head to fall to his father's shoulder.

About twenty minutes passed before a short, brown woman in pale green scrubs hurried through the sliding doors. She carried an electronic tablet and wore a stethoscope around her neck. "Blunt," she called.

Paulis and Roree rose and quickly walked over to her.

She extended her hand. "Hello I'm Dr. Patel. Are you Mr. Blunt?"

"Yes."

"Sarah is your wife?"

"Yes," Roree's eyes were drawn to the big sapphire jewel on her finger.

She glanced at Paulis and then nodded to the guard, who scanned his ID at the control panel, making the big glass doors fly apart. Roree followed her into the ER treatment area, with Paulis close behind. They stopped next to an empty gurney.

"As you know, your wife was in an automobile accident tonight. She's stable and resting now. We did x-rays and it doesn't appear that she fractured anything. She does have weakness in her muscles and some visual problems, which were a little concerning to me."

"What's wrong with her vision; did she hit her head?" asked Roree, trying to control his emotions.

"We're not sure, but it seems better now. She was wearing her seatbelt, thankfully. We're sending her up for a head and spine CT to make sure we haven't missed anything. I'll take you in to say hello before she goes up. She's been given some pain medication, so she may be a little groggy. Is she on any medications?"

"No."

"Is she allergic to anything?"

"No."

"Ok, Right." Dr. Patel led them through a maze of curtained cubicles, occasionally looking back to make sure they were keeping up. They stopped at cubicle 7B. Sarah was on her back, tucked in a blanket, with guardrails up on either side. She had visible bruises on the left side of her face and eye. Roree moved to his wife's side, gazing into her eyes.

"Roree," she whispered.

He grabbed her hand, being careful not to move it from her side. "Relax, Honey, we're here."

He grabbed Paulis's hand and pulled him to his mother's side. Paulis stood and stared not sure what to do or say. He had never seen his mother look so helpless. Paulis wondered why she wasn't moving. Was her neck broken; did she try to hurt herself?

Dr. Patel stood to the side, observing. "Ok Mr. Blunt, we're ready to take her up for her CT, and then she'll be admitted for observation. I'm going to have you go back to the waiting room and they will tell you what floor she's on in about half an hour."

They watched as Sarah's bed rolled away with the wheels hopping and spinning, leaving Paulis dizzy with confusion. He looked to his father, trying to gauge how he should be feeling. Then the smell of shit hovered in the air, which seemed out of place in such a large, open space.

"What's the CT for?" asked Paulis.

"They want to make sure she didn't hurt her neck."

"Dr. Patel said she was concerned about her being weak?" Paulis looked into his father's eyes, wondering why he wasn't answering his questions.

Roree and Paulis stood to the side as another patient was moved into Sarah's empty space.

"Paulis, don't worry. Dr. Patel is doing everything to make sure she's ok." Roree tried to give him a reassuring look, but he had questions of his own. He hugged Paulis as they followed the exit signs through the maze of hysteria and back to the waiting room.

Chapter 6

Roree sat with his son in the waiting room, consumed with thoughts about what was happening to his wife. Was there something he could have done to prevent this? Maybe he should have offered to take Vivian home? Subconsciously, the thought of being trapped in the car with that woman wasn't the slightest bit appealing to him. He was so wrapped up in his own work, that he hadn't thought of doing the right thing, and taking her home. He didn't want people thinking he didn't always do the right thing.

His thoughts shifted to the social ethics lecture he had given earlier that day. This class was always a challenge for him, because technology was continuously morphing this topic into un-chartered territory. The younger Ph.D.s had full blown theses predicting where society was headed. Though there was always a waitlist to get into his classes, staying ahead of the new generation of tech-savvy professors was his biggest challenge.

"Did everyone power down their phones?" asked Roree to the class.

There was a lukewarm response from the audience of two hundred students. "Ok good, because this room is wired to monitor energy fluctuations. Active cell phones can interfere with the signals and sometimes strange things happen."

Roree went to his computer and opened his first PowerPoint slide. "In this class we will explore the internet and its integral role in today's society. We'll take a broad look at domestic and global commerce. We will cover advertising, the ever-changing social networks, the porn industry, and medicine. But my special interest lies in what you guys are doing, and more importantly, what you're about to do."

Roree stood tall and scanned the room, making eye contact with his audience. A girl in the second row screamed and threw her cell phone on the floor. Shaking the heat from her hand, she watched as the smoking phone bounced down the aisle. Roree walked over to her and looked her in the eyes.

"There's no littering in my classroom." Suddenly, several cell phones began smoking as the chatter began to rise throughout the lecture hall.

"What did you do to our phones?" she demanded.

"Who said I did anything to your phone?"

"This is no coincidence," said the girl in the second row as she looked around the room furious. "What right do you have to destroy my phone!" she screamed.

Roree frowned and moved closer to her. "What right do you have to accuse me of anything, and what were you doing on the phone in the first place? Now sit down, or get out!" he shouted as he stiffly pointed to the door in the back of the room. Then he smiled and spoke with a sincere, nurturing tone. "Please have a seat. I have a new phone for you." He looked at the audience. "Anybody else whose phone has malfunctioned, please see me after class."

The entire room stopped moving and focused on Roree. "It looks like I now have your attention. Maybe I'll destroy your phone every time, or at least until someone of authority tells me I can't. Maybe I will just sell the rights to the technology I used, to a company looking to dominate the market over their competitors. I bet many of you would be interested in buying it. Maybe I had nothing to do with your phones undergoing a spontaneous combustion."

Roree smiled. "Look, I know texting and tweeting is like breathing for you people so feel free to do what you do. I just need you to take me along for the ride as we pick the entire concept apart." Roree went back to his PowerPoint slides. "There will be several extra credit research projects you will have the opportunity to participate in as the semester progresses. Of course, most will be voluntary, but I will pay you for projects that have an after-hours commitment. I will also supply you with cell phones and tablets as needed."

"As you probably know, the internet was designed to link the world via one common medium. Snail mail has become a thing of the past and we're saving trees. Though, saving trees and eliminating mail carrier jobs was not the goals, they are the rewards and the price of progress."

"Websites have become quite sophisticated and your personal data is usually secure. Investors can now access a business' financial statements with the click of a finger. But let's not be delusional. How do we gauge the level of trust we should instill in any source? This is the problem you guys need to solve."

"Any idiot, or should I say, any source with high-speed internet access can post an opinion, and we are clueless to what motivated the source. The internet fosters uninhibited social behavior. There's less honesty, less integrity and less accountability than what we see in person, in church, at work, or in our non-virtual communities."

"We couldn't adequately control society pre-internet, so adding another dimension via lightning speed fiber optics was bound to create a world where chaos, masked as innovation, could fester until…"

"Blunt!" The sound over the intercom interrupted his thoughts.

---The Expensive Scare Unit---

The receptionist called out, "Blunt!"

Roree was abruptly brought back to the emergency room, which was surprisingly calm. Paulis was asleep on his shoulder. Sweat had formed on his arm from Paulis's forehead. He looked at his watch; 3:10 a.m. "Fuck."

Roree eased Paulis's head from his shoulder and went to speak with the receptionist.

"Mr. Blunt, your wife was admitted to the intensive care unit on level four."

Roree didn't understand. "Intensive Care?"

"Yes, just head on up to the fourth floor and her physicians will answer all of your questions." She did not seem to be open to further discussion.

Roree and Paulis took the elevator up to the fourth floor. When the doors parted they were immediately engulfed with stillness and quiet. They saw a yellow sign pointing to the left reading "Neurology Intensive Care Unit." Roree double-checked the floor number, making sure they had reached the correct stop. As the two followed the yellow arrows down the long, high-ceilinged corridors, they finally reached a small open waiting room. Roree and Paulis entered the dimly lit room and walked up to the receptionist who was scanning information into the computer.

"Hello, I'm Dr. Blunt. I was told my wife is being admitted to this unit?"

"Yes, Dr. Blunt, she's here now. Go to the nursing station, and they will take care of you."

Paulis and Roree passed through the quiet waiting room and entered the ward. The buzz on this unit was just as intense as the ER, but it was controlled, under spoken, and very serious. It didn't take a medical degree to see that the people here were very ill, and required a great deal of care.

The Neuro Intensive Care Unit consisted of fifteen patient beds that surrounded a large, circular nursing station. The units were five times the size of the ones in the ER and had several monitors suspended from the ceiling and angled out from the beds. Paulis listened to the intrusive silence of his surroundings. He watched the rhythm of the lights and felt the peculiar surge of energy as it slowly maneuvered his innocence out from under his feet. Wearily, he drifted to his father's side and buried his head into his shoulder.

There was a team of physicians huddled at the head of one of the beds, checking the charts, analyzing the hanging IV bags and discussing their observations. Finally, one of the physicians gave instructions to the charge nurse, as the rest of the team moved onto the next bed. It seemed like a well-oiled machine, with techs in white coats making sure all the individual pieces were functioning properly, but the reality was the patients here were fighting for their lives.

Paulis was wide awake, looking from bed to bed, trying to find his mother. He thought, there must be a mistake. His mother didn't seem sick enough to be in this place.

One of the nurses called out as she stepped from behind the desk. "Mr. Blunt."

Roree turned his attention to her and Paulis continued at his side.

"Mr. Blunt, they're almost done with rounds; the doctor will be with you in a moment."

"Ok," said Roree.

Dr. Lee was the attending physician covering the ICU tonight. He enjoyed the pace of the ICU because he got to see a variety of exciting cases, without the turnover typically seen in the ER. Neurology and the body's wiring were Dr. Lee's real fancy.

The body sends signals to your muscles and they respond. You feel fire on your hand, and instinctively jerk your hand away. There doesn't always have to be an associated, conscious thought process. Sometimes the body just takes what it needs. The challenge comes when the body "thinks" it's doing what it needs to do and starts taking when it's not necessary.

The body is designed to protect itself from foreign substances. When things are disrupted and the body fails to distinguish what is foreign from that which is native, an autoimmune process is said to be underway. A body at war can launch an attack upon itself that can reduce a healthy person to a twitching ball of chaos. Dr. Lee's job was to reintroduce the dynamic equilibrium that was disrupted during such a war.

As Dr. Lee approached, Roree noted that he seemed to be in a good mood, considering all the sickness around him and the time of the morning.

"Mr. Blunt, I'm Dr. Lee. I will be caring for your wife while she's here. How are you and your son holding up?"

Roree was immediately taken aback by his heavy British accent, noting that nothing appeared as it seemed in this place. "I think I'd feel better if someone told me why my wife needs to be on this unit!"

This was the third distressed family Dr. Lee had counseled that night, but he was intent on providing this family with the care they deserved. "I know you haven't been told much about your wife's condition. We've been trying to get a handle on what's going on with her."

Dr. Lee gave Paulis a reassuring look. "She's stable. As you know, she was admitted to the ER tonight after having an automobile accident. It doesn't look like she broke anything. Fortunately she was wearing her seatbelt, but she was unconscious when the paramedics brought her in. When she regained consciousness she was able to describe a bit of what happened, but she was having some visual problems and muscle weakness.

"What did she say happened?" asked Roree.

"She said she temporarily lost her eyesight, and when it came back, she didn't have time to prevent the accident."

"Is she blind?" asked Paulis.

"No her vision has returned. We did some imaging of her head, neck and back to check for nerve damage. We didn't find any acute damage related to the accident. However, we did see what looks like demyelination in parts of her brain."

"Demyelination?" Roree frowned.

"Yes, myelin is like a protective coating on the nerves of the brain, which allows it to function normally."

Roree frowned again and his stomach began to stir.

Dr. Lee noted the bruise on Roree's cheek. "We admitted her here because her muscle weakness has progressed since she arrived, and if her breathing becomes a problem this is the best place to handle that type of thing."

"What do her muscles have to do with her breathing?" asked Roree.

Dr. Lee animatedly held his hands just above his stomach. "The diaphragm is just a big muscle, so if it's weak, it can affect your breathing." He carefully touched Roree's shoulder. "I don't think it will be of concern. When was her last doctor's appointment?"

"I guess it's been about six months, and she was fine. She got new glasses yesterday. She was having problems with her eyes. Other than that, she didn't have any health problems."

Dr. Lee gave Roree an inquisitive look. "I see. Has she ever had problems with muscle weakness?"

"No."

"Right. I'd like to do a spinal tap to rule out infections and get a special MRI. We'll continue the steroids, and refer her for genetic testing to see if we can't get some clear answers to what's happening."

"Ok, can we see her now?" asked Roree as he impatiently moved into the room.

Paulis pulled away from his father, sniffling. "What's wrong with her? You're leaving something out!"

Dr. Lee spoke calmly. "We believe there's a problem with her nerves that's making her muscles weak. This may have caused her to have the accident."

Paulis was speaking softly now. "Is she gonna die?"

Dr. Lee gently rubbed the back of Paulis's shoulder. "No, I think we can treat her, but we need a little more information. Try not to worry. We're keeping a close eye on your mother." He exchanged a glance with Paulis and Roree and began moving towards Sarah's bed. "Any other questions?"

Paulis gave Dr. Lee a blank stare as he led the Blunts over to Sarah's cubicle. Roree and Paulis stood by Sarah's bed as they prepared to roll her off for her MRI. Sarah looked pale and weak, barely able to move her hand in response to her husband's touch. She felt her thighs quiver with confusion as the pain shot from her hips to the balls of her feet. Every time it happened, nothing else mattered, and she was reminded that this long night was not interested in reason. She looked up at her boys as a tear streaked to her ear.

"Sarah; don't be scared, it will be over soon," said Roree.

"I'm not scared, I'm just happy that you're both here for me."

Roree smiled, wiped her tears and gave her a kiss on the lips.

As she was being rolled away she called out. "Call Mother, and let her know what's happening." Roree exhaled heavily as he watched her being taken away once again.

---The MRI---

"This is not the time to be claustrophobic," Sarah thought to herself, as she was carefully loaded into the scanner.

A voice came over the speaker. "Ok, hold still and we'll get this done quickly."

The sounds started around her slender, even-toned frame. "Clink, clank, clink, clank..." Sarah tried to focus on the happy place her mother had described to her as a child, whenever she was anxious. Her happy place was on vacation in Honolulu with her parents before the nasty divorce, where her mother drove her father away. She had fond memories of lying on the beach and sipping from a coconut, while watching her parents playfully flirt with each other.

Now her happy place was competing with the chill blowing up her flimsy hospital gown, and then there was the question of what had they done with her purse? It was difficult for her to block the horrible reality this place brought to light.

She couldn't remember anything that happened between the accident and waking up in the ER. While heading home on I-93 Sarah's central vision abruptly became fuzzy. As it cleared up, she saw that she was approaching a sharp turn, but when she tried to adjust the car, it swerved. Her right foot was all pins and needles, and though she managed to get her foot on the brake, she was not sure if her foot was unable to successfully push the brake, or if the brakes just failed. The next thing she knew, the car was spinning like a deadly toy.

What if they took her driver's license away? How was she going to get around and take care of her husband and child? What about her job and her aging mother? What if something horrible was happening to her? She had a cracking headache, and her eyes had begun to burn and water again. Sarah started to swallow and sniffle.

A voice came on. "Hold still, we're nearly done."

---Hospital Release---

After nine days, Sarah was finally being released from the hospital. Her anxiety level was high, not knowing how she would function at home. She had regained the use of her limbs, but still experienced occasional weakness, and considered her muscles unreliable. The geneticist was scheduled to meet with her to review her test results, earlier, but never turned up. Sarah was about to call the nurses' station to find out what the hold-up was when the doctor finally arrived.

Dr. Babette Jones casually entered her room, wearing what looked like an evening gown under a crisp, white lab coat. Her long, shiny, black hair was caught under the collar of her coat. Despite the youthful, flirty energy, Sarah could see the age in her face. Her lips were pouty and full. Her chocolate skin was well preserved for her advanced age. Sarah envisioned herself with such a demeanor if she continued to take good care of herself.

Dr. Jones approached, having skillfully examined Sarah's posture before reaching her bedside. This doctor's inquisitive gaze made her nervous. Sarah tried to control her breathing but to no avail, as she knew she was being observed.

"Hello Sarah, I'm Dr. Jones. I bet you're ready to get out of here?"

Sarah exhaled and smiled awkwardly.

"Don't worry; I didn't come to poke and prod. I'm sure you've already had enough of that. I just need your consent to contact your family so I can finish compiling your genetic profile."

"Of course," said Sarah as she reached for the forms.

"I'm also going to need contact information for your parents."

"Well, I haven't had much contact with my father since I was a child, but I'm sure my mother would know how to reach him, if she really wanted to." Sarah cringed as she thought about the steep cost she would incur to get Vivian to agree to such a request.

"Excellent. That would be great, and what about your mother?" Dr. Jones had moved in closer to her bed.

"My mother gave her background information after I was admitted. It should be in the chart." Sarah became aware of the pillow against her back, as Dr. Jones nonchalantly hovered in her personal space.

"I meant your biological mother." As she spoke, Dr. Jones felt as if she had swallowed the worm from the bottom of a tequila bottle; surprised by its rough, fluffy texture, yet weary of its unpredictable effects.

"She *is* my biological mother!" said Sarah, confused.

“Oh. Well, I noticed that your blood types were incompatible, so I assumed that you were adopted.” Dr. Jones focused on Sarah and lowered her voice, allowing it to fade off in amazement. “At your age I assumed you knew ...”

Sarah stared straight ahead, in shock.

Dr. Jones smiled apologetically. “I’ll double check the information, I’m sure there must have been a typo, somewhere.”

“What did my mother say her blood type was?”

“She’s Type O and you’re Type AB.” Babette paused and then continued. “As a biologist, I’m sure you see my dilemma. Anyway, I’ll let you know how the study is coming along and I will make my results available to your neurologist, so he can tailor your treatment plan accordingly.”

Sarah continued to stare, not hearing a word the doctor said as her world began to churn. Dr. Jones reached back, tucked her forearm under her hair and whipped it out from under the collar of her coat. She then turned and left the room.

Sarah’s head spun slowly, as if she were caught in a reluctant tail spin. Is it possible that her mother kept this secret from her, all this time? It would explain why her father found it so easy to stay out of her life. Sarah began to feel very alone and betrayed.

When she recovered from her thoughts the nurse had arrived with a wheelchair in preparation for her discharge from the facility. Roree was on his way to rescue her from this never-ending nightmare.

Chapter 7

Almost two weeks had passed since Sarah's diagnosis. Paulis had just arrived for his afternoon chemistry lab, and was awaiting instructions from the professor. Most of the other students had already arrived and were chatting and swiping at the benches in front of them, reviewing the Dimension's website.

Paulis was seated at the bench in the back of the room when Terry entered. Several people waved as she walked in, searching for Paulis. She was striking, at five-foot nine inches, with a very confident stride and delicate, smooth skin for a teenager. She had on a black, knee-length skirt; black, knee high-leather boots, and a sweater with playful water colors. She smiled and shyly waved as she hunched forward, lugging the weight of her backpack to the back of the room.

She was out of breath. "Hey, what's the download. Did I miss anything?"

"No." Paulis helped her remove her backpack.

She tugged on her lab coat and balanced her protective goggles on her head. "Paulis why are we all the way back here?"

Paulis quietly drank in the smell of her perfume and everything about her. "I like to keep some distance between me and authority." They both laughed.

"So, what's up with you?"

Terry shrugged her shoulders. "I'm ok I guess; I'm here. All things considered, I'm feeling pretty good." She smiled. "How's your mother doing?"

"Better. She just got released from the hospital yesterday. She's still weak, but her eyes are back to normal."

"What's wrong with her eyes? I thought you said she has MS."

"She does. Optic neuritis is part of that."

"Oh, well I'm glad to hear she's getting back to normal."

"Me, too." Paulis gave her a quiet, desperate look. "I'm happy we're becoming friends. I wasn't sure that would happen."

Terry batted her eyes at him. "Let me guess. Is it because of my IQ?"

Paulis was a little shocked by her candor. "Well, yes, and because of mine." He laughed to himself.

Professor Reynolds looked in their direction, a little annoyed, as he had begun instruction on the day's lab procedure. He continued his discussion on fluid dynamics, pressure, heat, and semi-permeable membranes, and how they relate to the body.

"Don't believe the hype. I'm just a beautiful black woman with a big ass brain. I've been told the breasts will come later." They both laughed.

Then her mood changed a bit. "Of course, I may have to cut them off with the BRCA-1 breast cancer gene hanging over my head. My mother has never had a problem, but I can tell she's a little anxious about it. Of course, she's anxious about a lot of things."

Professor Reynolds looked in their direction again, but continued. "By a show of hands, did everyone complete their downloads last night?" First a few hands went up, then everyone raised their hands. "Always remember to get a full night's sleep to ensure that you successfully convert the new information from your short-term memory to your long-term memory. If you're experiencing anxiety, not sleeping well, or having odd dreams, it's probably normal. But please be sure to discuss it during your bi-weekly counseling sessions with the translational therapist." He looked at his young group with pride. "Good. So now you have the first 10 chapters of the book tucked away in your brains. I'm not saying get rid of your books, but we'll get there soon enough. Has anyone been able to access the information?"

No hands were raised.

"Ok you're gonna need to make an effort, or you're just wasting space here," said Professor Reynolds.

Terry was silent as she thought about how she almost ended up in private school last year. She was initially declined acceptance to Dimensions, because the school was under the impression that her parents were not supportive of her genetic test results. More specifically, they were not supportive of the possibility of her being gay. Then, suddenly, her parents claimed to have warmed up to the possibility, though she still had her doubts. She knew her parents thought that their support was critical for her success. They behaved as though her accomplishments were a direct reflection of their competency as parents. They figured her future successes would negate the damage done by her potential gayness. Unfortunately, love was not necessarily part of that equation. Her grandmother had always been supportive, and she was also on the admissions board for Dimensions, which made it all the more puzzling when she was rejected.

Terry raised her hand. "I think I have access?"

Professor Reynolds energetically extended his hands to Terry. "Ok Dear, tell us about it."

"I was reading the cereal box and I noticed that it had chemical formulas on it. Somehow, I knew exactly what they were, and I could even see their three dimensional structures in my head. Then I started to think about other compounds and I tried writing them out, but my head started to spin, so I stopped."

"Excellent; the download is designed to be put to use, but blatant regurgitation is a brain strain, and may give you a headache. So, yes the information is there, and once you've used it in a practical setting, you will always have access to it. Remember, trying to upload the information to an unauthorized device is a copyright violation."

"Is that what happened to Shelly?" asked Isaiah, from the front row.

"No, Shelly wasn't supposed to start receiving downloads until her second year, like the rest of you."

"I heard she's still in a coma," said Terry, in an accusatory tone. She could never resist the opportunity to articulate herself in front of her peers. Being an only child, Terry had learned how to command an audience. At first it was a row of teddy bears, followed by an assortment of Barbie dolls, and then she graduated to the neighborhood kids. Dimensions was her new playground.

Professor Reynolds walked to the center of the lab. "Her access logs indicated that she hacked in and downloaded information without our permission. Now, I'm really not at liberty to discuss the details of this unfortunate incident. Just follow the rules, and I assure you, by the time you graduate, you'll be able to study at the institution of your choice."

Professor Reynolds moved back to the front of the room and searched the students for more comments while noting the silent concern in their eyes.

"How do you know what to expect, if you've never actually had a download yourself?" asked Isaiah.

Professor Reynolds always had problems taking Isaiah seriously because he was a sagger; one of those kids who couldn't be bothered to pull his pants all the way up. "Why do you assume that I haven't had a download?" asked Professor Reynolds. "It just so happens that our experiment is about that very thing; taking only the information we've actually observed as fact and then drawing the most reasonable conclusion. Observing the dynamics of fluid is a good start toward understanding how the body responds to pressure, and other conditions."

"In front of you are several sets of conditions upon which you will make observations, and based on those observations draw conclusions. When you're done here, you and your partner are to construct a hypothesis, explaining what you think the experiments prove, and how it relates to fluid dynamics. Don't forget to discuss your experimental error, as well. Tomorrow, we will review your hypotheses, and correct any areas where your thought processes have failed you."

The class giggled, and Paulis raised his hand. "It seems like we would get more out of the experiment if you explained it before we did it?"

"Mr. Blunt, I'm not interested in your ability to regurgitate facts or follow a recipe. Perhaps it will be you who sees something no one else has ever seen. I want to know how you think when you're not given any facts. I want you to close your mouth, open your eyes, and make sense of what's on the table in front of you."

Then he turned to the entire class. "I'm going to need you all to start wearing your protective head guards when you're in public, now that you're receiving downloads. Don't worry, they look cool," said Professor Reynolds sarcastically. "We need to work together through this process as a team, and in the end, we will beat them all."

"Ok everybody, let's do some work!"

Paulis was feeling a little embarrassed, thinking maybe he had asked a stupid question. He searched Terry's, eyes trying to see if she had detected his embarrassment.

"Quite honestly, I didn't think a guy like you would want to talk to me, because of my genetics," said Terry.

Paulis reflected a moment, a little surprised that she wanted to discuss this. "So, are you gay?"

"Not yet; I keep waiting for the day when I wake up lusting after Tyra Banks, but it's just not happening."

“What about Ellen DeGeneres? I think she might be a more appropriate litmus test.” They both laughed. The instructor paused and looked over in their direction.

“Everybody wants to know if I’m gay,” whispered Terry. “Don’t get me wrong, nobody’s rude or vicious. Let’s face it; the school wouldn’t put up with that kind of blatant ignorance, so who knows what they really think. I just think it’s interesting how people assume so much about who you are, based on one abstract piece of information. Now, on the real, the girls are all guarded around me, and guys are just not interested.”

“Well I’m interested.”

Terry gave him a quiet smile. “Me too.”

The professor had made his way to the back of the room, in the direction of their bench. “I’m sure it’s all very important, but I require your undivided attention. Nothing else!” The professor then turned and walked away.

The room was silent, and all eyes were on them. Paulis looked at the professor like a deer caught in headlights, but Terry aggressively stared him down as he walked away. “You do realize you work for us!” said Terry emphatically.

“Spoken like a girl itching to go back to private school,” said Professor Reynolds without looking back.

Terry didn't respond. She wasn't sure why she was being so disrespectful towards Professor Reynolds. Since she started receiving the downloads, she had been having a rush of thoughts and emotions. Sometimes, she spoke before she thought it through, and it was starting to cause problems. Her mouth was spewing out raw, unfiltered truth, but not everybody was ready for the truth, not even Professor Reynolds.

Chapter 8

The wind huffed the runaway leaves to and fro, as if hypnotized by a manic pied piper. The afternoon had faded, but it was earlier than it seemed. Roree was still surprised at how dark it was when his 4:00 p.m. lecture ended. The smell of winter was in the air. He loved everything about winter, except the people who incessantly whined about it. He thought they should leave New England, if they felt it was so unbearable. He recalled the long winter weekends skiing with his parents during his high school years. The bone chilling hills of snow would pull him through the course, leaving him breathless, with his parents trailing but refusing to be left behind. He felt alive and in control during this stage of his life. He regretted never taking Paulis for a riveting adventure on the slopes, but he wanted something more substantial for his child.

Roree was home at the computer in the study, lost in thought. He was entranced by the oversized, HD holographic monitors, and the images projecting from within. Now that he was officially on the team to create and push the new internet initiative forward, the pressure was weighing heavily on him to produce results.

Many of the parents volunteered their time and financial resources to keep Dimensions among the premier New England institutions of higher learning. The school had come a long way in regaining its public image after last year's tragedy. Sarah was on the wellness committee, but was feeling guilty that she allowed her vaccine project to fall so far behind.

Sarah was on the bed, balancing Roree's laptop on her thighs while editing his lecture slides and catching up on the bills that had accumulated during her hospital stay. The down comforter felt nice and cool under her muscles, but she was already growing tired of the confines of this room. It wasn't giving off the cheery, healing vibe she needed.

The décor of the bedroom was the work of a minimalist. There were four tall, narrow oak dressers against the wall, and a couple of large, antique Persian rugs. The bed was a simple, wood slab of contemporary Italian design, supporting an oversized mattress. She was happy to be in familiar surroundings while getting her world back under control. However, she was still aware of her inability to escape her new reality.

Sarah was tired of being the sick woman but was still undeniably fatigued and very weak. The unpredictable throbbing sensations that seemed to arise from her joints and subsequently engulf her limbs, were debilitating at times. How could the Lord Almighty have created such a condition? She thought that life was a product of cause and effect. You did what you were supposed to do, and then you reaped the rewards of a good life. You went to the right schools, married the right guy, lived a healthy lifestyle and prosperity would be derived. It was all bullshit! What they didn't tell you is that the world isn't cut and dry, the surface is never what it seems, and the dimensions are fucked up on many levels. This was quite a lesson to learn at forty-three, and was of no comfort to her this evening. She knew it could happen to anyone, but it was happening to her. Once she got over this realization, there would be no more surprises. Her disease's main lesson was that life is unpredictable.

Sarah knew that feeling sorry for herself was not the answer. She wouldn't wallow in self-pity for long because that wasn't her style, but today she would own it. She planned to cry and embrace her horrible numb limbs, though at times she could not identify their position. Today she would feel the angst, with the expectation that tomorrow would be different. Tomorrow she would be different.

Roree had just begun to construct a new web page when he received a text message. He looked at the screen, and saw it was from Sarah.

"Are you home? I'm hungry. Do you mind bringing me my medication from the refrigerator and some of that leftover Chinese food?"

Roree thought about how behind he was on his project. He saved his work on the computer, labeling it as "Behavior Modification via System Disabling Virus" and then went down to the kitchen, mumbling to himself. "Do I mind? As if that's even relevant!"

Roree entered the room with a tray containing a plate of Chinese food, her medication injection pen, and a glass of water. The shades were drawn, and there was a sour odor in the air. He moved over to the bed and took the computer from Sarah's lap, replacing it with the tray of food. Then he opened the shades and cracked a window, allowing the fresh air to engage the room.

Sarah smiled. "Thank you, Dear. How long have you been home?"

Roree gave her a delicate kiss on the forehead. "You're welcome."

Sarah observed that he hadn't kissed her on the lips since she got home from the hospital. She was feeling helpless, like her emotions were lying exposed and trembling. She needed to feel desired, though sex was the last thing on her mind. Maybe it was the steroids she was on that made her feel this way. Roree sat on the bed next to her, and began scanning through his lecture slides while she shoveled Kung Pao chicken into her face.

The room was quiet except for Roree's clicking and Sarah's chewing. Sarah was slightly dazed as she watched the food move from the plate to her mouth, feeling the delightful sensations burst from her taste buds; one of the few pleasures not stripped away by her disease. She had put on about fifteen pounds in the last couple of weeks. She didn't like taking the steroids, though they seemed to control the pain and irritation. She was afraid of getting infections while her immune system was being suppressed, and then, of course, she had read about the possibility of her bones thinning if she took the steroids for an extended period of time.

Roree looked over at his wife. “Didn’t I ask you to use size thirty-two font for all the PowerPoint slides?”

She paused from her meal, thinking about how she had spent the last few hours correcting his atrocious spelling. “Roree, the nurse aides left my medications in the bathroom. Could you please bring them to me? I should take them with my shot, after I’m done with my meal.”

He gave her a sympathetic look. “Of course; how are you feeling today?”

“My muscles are not as weak this afternoon, so I think the medications are working. My physical therapist is coming tomorrow. I could be back to work in no time.”

“That’s great!”

“I hope you haven’t been feeding Paulis takeout the entire time I was away. He’s a growing boy, and he needs a home-cooked meal.”

“Don’t we all,” said Roree.

Sarah looked at him in disbelief.

“He’s fine. He’s certainly happy that you’re home. He’s worried about you.”

“Too bad he couldn’t be more like you,” said Sarah.

“What’s that supposed to mean?” Roree couldn’t understand where all of this hostility was coming from.

Sarah paused and examined his face for a moment. “I have an appointment with the neurologist this Friday at 10:30 a.m.”

“I’m scheduled to present my web design to the committee Friday afternoon,” said Roree.

“Roree, I need you to be there. The only other appointment was late next week.”

“Sarah, if you need me to go, I will!”

“I was hoping you would *want* to go!”

“Next time, let me know before scheduling an appointment.”

They breathed heavily, both quiet for a moment. Sarah went back to eating, feeling her arms begin to weigh with fatigue. Roree went back to his lecture slides.

“Roree, my medications?”

“Oh, sorry.” Roree went to the bathroom and returned with her pills.

Paulis was home, rummaging through the refrigerator, but he finally settled for an apple from the big bowl on the table. He could see from the living room that the lights were on in the study, so he went upstairs, looking for his parents. Paulis saw that the computer was on but the room was empty. He turned to head out of the study, and ran into his father.

"Hey, where's Mother?"

Roree looked at the computer monitors, and then Paulis. "She's in the bedroom. When did you get home?"

Paulis walked past him into the hallway, taking a bite out of the apple. "I just got here." Paulis continued down the long corridor, entering the master bedroom.

"Hey, how's it going?" He went over and plucked a piece of chicken from his mother's plate.

"I'm fine. Did you wash your hands?"

He smiled and licked his fingers. "No."

"Oh my God, I'm raising a heathen!"

Paulis laughed, and grabbed another piece of chicken.

Sarah admired her growing boy for a moment. His shoulders had started to broaden and his peach fuzz was thickening. It looked like he had started ironing his jeans. "Paulis, I'm sorry I haven't been here to take care of you. This must be difficult for you to handle."

He observed his mother's uncombed hair and the medications by the bed, as she laid there in her pajamas in the middle of the day. He couldn't recall a moment where she was not in control. He had to look away, for fear that his watery eyes would deceive him.

He laughed. "You know, I'm old enough to handle myself. Is there something I can do to help out?"

Sarah smiled with pride as she took her son's hand. Some day he was going to be a powerful man she thought to herself. "I'm going to have good days and bad days. Just remember that I'll always be here for you. It's comforting to know that you're here for me too."

Paulis felt her dry, spongy hand tremble as she squeezed. He squeezed back watching her face to make sure he wasn't hurting her. "I am here for you," he said. "I want you to visit YouTube and watch a series of videos about people living with MS. It could help you to see how others are coping with the same illness."

"Ok Honey, I'll check it out."

With that, Paulis went to his room to begin his evening study session.

Later that evening, Sarah awoke from her nap to a pitch-black room and the urge to urinate. Her muscles were feeling stronger and she was confident that between the upcoming physical therapy and her compliance with the drug regimen, she could keep this disease under control.

She turned on the lamp, and got up to go to the bathroom. When she got away from the bed, she caught a toenail on the fringes of the area rug, making her stumble. Her arms flew out, and her neck snapped down by reflex, to steady her position. Then she received numbing sensations down her back and her knees buckled, sending her toppling forward. She landed hard, bashing the side of her face on the edge of the dresser, and then she collapsed on her rib cage. Her embarrassment quickly faded as a stinging bruise rose on her cheek. She lay there, with the wind knocked out of her, holding the side of her head.

"Roree!!" she screamed, then began to sob quietly.

Both Paulis and Roree came running into the bedroom. Roree saw her on the floor crying and ran over to her.

He lifted her up from behind by her arms and helped her to the bathroom as Paulis stood to the side. "You ok?" asked Roree.

"Ouch, you're hurting me-careful under my arms!"

"Sarah, you're trying to do too much, too soon! You should have called me if you needed help."

She looked back at him without the energy or patience to explain what happened. "Asshole!"

For a brief moment, Sarah reminded Roree of her mother. His eyes widened as he thought to himself, wondering what he had done to deserve that.

Chapter 9

It had been several days since Sarah's fall. Vivian had been staying at the house to help ensure her daughter's safety when the home health care workers were away. At first it was every day, but now it was with less frequency, since Sarah's muscle strength had improved. Vivian pretended that it was a burden on her, but she liked taking care of her flesh and blood. Her family was important to her, and it gave her a sense of purpose and control. After retiring from the law firm, she had only taken on a pro bono case here and there, so it was nice for her to be busy again.

Paulis was in the kitchen with Sarah and Vivian. He was intoxicated by the aroma of the pot roast, and Vivian's heavy garlic hand. He had received a text message and eagerly checked his phone. Moments later the door bell rang, and Paulis jumped up in excitement. He paused, and skillfully tucked his dreadlocks into place before opening the door.

Terry entered his home, looking even prettier than she did the last time he saw her. She could be a model if she wanted, he thought to himself. He was tempted to touch the fur collar on her blue jean jacket just to get closer but decided against it. She pivoted her body, looking around the big, glass room. "Oh Paulis, I love your home, it's very cool." She stopped in the middle of the room, drawn to the big colorful paintings hanging from the walls. She felt like she was in a contemporary art museum. Abstract art was everything and nothing, and she loved it!

Paulis paused, impatiently waiting for her to disconnect from the provocative artwork. “Yes, I know. You can tell me what you think, later.” Paulis tugged her moist hand and led her to the kitchen.

“This is Terry, my lab partner,” announced Paulis, trying to contain his smile.

Vivian and Sarah offered greetings. Terry nodded and smiled uncomfortably as she quickly scanned the room, noticing Sarah’s unearthly beauty. Sarah reminded her of her own grandmother, poised like a warrior, despite the four-pronged cane propped behind her chair. Next, Terry observed the handsome, elderly woman running the kitchen, and understood that Paulis’s good looks were supported by a strong lineage.

Sarah gazed inquisitively as she tried to assess Terry’s understanding of their family dynamics.

Terry inhaled deeply, savoring the aromas in the kitchen. “Something smells nice.”

Vivian smiled. “Honey, you’re welcome to stay for dinner, if you like.”

Paulis quickly threw his hand up. “No thanks Grandma, we’re just gonna study. We have a lot of work to do.”

Vivian intently postured toward Paulis's young companion. "I insist! You can study until dinner is ready, and then take a break. Isn't that standard protocol around here?" asked Vivian sarcastically.

Terry met her gaze. "Thanks, it's very nice of you to offer but…"

"Good, then it's settled," said Vivian.

"Make sure you call your mother and let her know you're having dinner here," added Sarah.

"Ok, I will." Terry wasn't sure what had just happened, but judging by Paulis's reaction, he wasn't ready for her to get too close to his family. She supposed he hadn't told them about her genetic variations.

Paulis rolled his eyes and led Terry out of the kitchen. "My grandmother has a forked tongue," whispered Paulis.

"Oh my God, that's an awful thing to say about your grandmother!"

Paulis snickered. "You can't say I didn't warn you."

Paulis gave her a tour of the house, demonstrating how the self-cleaning bathrooms worked, and spending a little time discussing the art, before finally going upstairs to his room to study.

Vivian slid on the oven mitts and carefully removed her roast from the oven. She looked over her shoulder at Sarah, avoiding the steam that whooshed from the pan as she uncovered it. "She's a pretty girl, and sharp too," said Vivian.

"Yes, Paulis has good taste."

"I thought he might follow his mother's lead and pick a Caucasian."

"Well apparently he takes after his father," said Sarah.

"You'd better keep an eye on that boy. Teenage boys are nothing but hormones." She frowned, sucking through her teeth, and then drained her wine glass. "The rising flesh is not to be taken lightly. You need to keep tabs on those children."

"Mother, let me worry about my son's flesh, and you focus on your roast."

"I'm just saying my piece, but I've seen those sheets of his. The Lord works in the supernatural. He looks after the young and stupid, but thou who shall not see."

"Mother, my eyes are just fine, they should be with all the steroids I'm taking." They both laughed.

"Yes, I see you've put on a couple of pounds, too," said Vivian, as she moved toward the refrigerator.

Sarah looked at her ample bosom and closed her eyes, rubbing them gently, as if to erase her mother's insensitive comments.

Vivian called from the refrigerator, "Don't you have anything else, other than this Trader Joe's wine?"

"No, that's all that we have."

"Blasphemy!" Vivian laughed as she steadied her trembling hands to open the bottle. She poured herself another glass of wine, and joined Sarah at the table. Vivian elegantly took a sip. "So, where is Roree tonight?"

Sarah's eyes casually lingered on Vivian's glass for a moment. "He had an afternoon lecture, but he should be home in time for dinner."

"Are you sure?" Vivian watched her daughter, wondering when she was going to examine the evidence that sat before her.

"If he didn't it would be horribly deceitful of him, wouldn't it?" said Sarah, as she thought about how the woman sitting across from her had been lying to her for all these years. Keeping such a secret from her was unforgivable. However, Sarah was afraid to ask for the truth, because she wasn't ready to deal with it. She could handle her distant husband, her teenage boy with raging hormones, and the uncertainty of her MS. It was her own truth, and the rewriting of history, that was too much to bear.

Sarah felt a little nauseous, and her bladder began to contract. “Mother, could you help me to the bathroom?”

“Oh, touché,” said Vivian as she carefully sat her wine glass down. Then she got up, gave Sarah her cane, and stepped to the side.

Sarah looked up at her, trying not to panic. “Mother, I’m in a bit of a hurry!”

“I guess you shouldn’t have waited until the last minute to ask for help.” Vivian stepped a little closer but did not reach out. Sarah clenched her abdominal muscles, locking her bladder into place, and carefully maneuvered out of the chair, balancing on her cane. She slowly made her way to the bathroom, with Vivian shadowing closely behind.

“You know what they say, once a man, twice a child,” said Vivian.

“Don’t worry Mother, I’m sure you’ll get your turn.”

Sarah and Vivian were finally seated in the living room when Roree arrived. “I’m glad you made it home. We have a dinner guest tonight,” said Sarah.

“Great; hello, Vivian.” Roree waved at Vivian and gave Sarah a kiss on the forehead. “Who?”

"Paulis's cute little study partner," said Sarah.

"Oh, this should be interesting, I thought she was a figment of his imagination," said Roree. He noticed that Vivian's wig was off center, there was a bead of sweat on her forehead, and her lipstick was misaligned, giving her a three-dimensional look. He exchanged an awkward glance with her and headed off to the study.

Paulis and Terry were in his room, working at the computer. He was acutely aware of Terry's presence. He struggled to ignore the suffocating heat generated by the proximity of her thigh. It was distracting him from the chemical formulas on the screen.

"Paulis, you should know this by now."

"I know, I'm getting it bit by bit."

"You don't have to memorize it," she said, tapping her finger on his temple. "Just try to apply the concepts and then you can derive the information that's already there. Do you think your downloads were successful?"

"Yes, the information is there, but it's kind of like there's another program running in the background. It's not intrusive, but when I try to focus, I can tell that it's pulling on my energy."

"So, let it go and stop trying to control it!"

Paulis smiled to himself as his abdomen relaxed. "I know, just keep going."

Chapter 10

At 7:00 sharp, Paulis and Terry went downstairs to join Sarah, Roree and Vivian, who were already seated at the table.

Sarah looked at the sterling silver mesh head guards strapped to the kids' heads. They covered the neck, chin, and most of the lower posterior skull. "You two need to remove those things from your heads before sitting at the dinner table."

"Mother, everybody's doing it."

"Not at the dinner table. Besides, you never know when I might need to connect with the backside of your head." Sarah smiled.

They got up from the table to remove their head guards, and quickly returned for dinner.

"So, how did you kids meet?" asked Vivian as they took their seats.

Paulis rolled his eyes. "We're not kids anymore!"

"Yes, I know, you think you're all grown up now," said Vivian, playfully.

"We met in the cafeteria, and she's in my chemistry class."

Terry was a little uncomfortable, because all eyes were on her. She was still wondering if Paulis had told them everything about her background. She wondered if this was a tenuous acceptance based on her flawless first impression, only to later be replaced by hatred and alienation, due to her genetic time bombs.

"Oh chemistry, that sounds interesting," said Roree.

"Mr. Blunt, I hear you're a sociology research professor," said Terry with admiration. "What's that like?"

"Please, call me Roree. Sociology is an interesting field these days. I'm also an expert with internet IP tracking and upload intervention technology." Terry noticed Vivian's eyes dart off as Roree continued. "The internet has created a society that your generation has embraced, as if it were part of your DNA."

Sarah laughed out loud. "Is that how you open your lectures?"

"Honey you should know; after all, you're the one creating all of his lecture slides," said Vivian, as she playfully glanced at Terry. "You know in her spare time she's a biology professor."

"Oh, I didn't know that," said Terry, catching Paulis's glance.

Roree continued. "I'm currently working on a project involving internet culture and ways to regulate and alter some of the more undesirable behaviors."

"Like what?" asked Terry.

"You know, predators and bullying. How would you feel if you could be held accountable for all of your actions when you send a text or Tweet? For example, if you send an angry text message to your mother, she could slow down the speed of your phone's operating system, or improve it to reward good behavior."

"I guess I wouldn't mind, if the person controlling my operating system didn't have her own dysfunctional agenda, that fluctuated based on her current dose," said Terry.

Vivian picked up her glass of wine. "Oh ride or die; I like this one!" Paulis and Terry laughed, but Roree didn't see what was so funny. "So, who's gonna control *your* phone, Roree?" asked Vivian.

Roree had fleeting images of his boot delicately resting on Vivian's exposed throat as his pulse rate jumped and he clenched his knuckles to a bloodless white. But he didn't utter a word.

"I'm sure you've heard all about my MS by now?" asked Sarah.

Terry followed Sarah's sad eyes. "Of course I have, and we've discussed it at school, but I have no idea what it's like. It sounds very challenging."

"Yes, I guess you could call it that. It's unpredictable, and I certainly wouldn't wish it on anyone."

"Do you believe this follows Darwin's Theory of Evolution and Natural Selection?" asked Paulis.

Sarah looked at him, a little shocked by the insensitivity of his question, but managed to find the innocence at its root. "Paulis, my illness may shorten the span of my life, but it hasn't inhibited my ability to reproduce."

"Maybe, but you're not likely to have as many kids with MS, so your ability to reproduce hasn't been *totally* inhibited, but it's been reduced. I think Paulis is correct." Terry smiled, and then felt her words reverberate against her forehead, making her wish she could take them back.

Vivian tucked her displaced bob behind her ear, flashing her glimmering ear stud, as she glanced between Roree and Sarah.

"So, Paulis, I guess one day, many years from now, you're going to have to give me lots of grandbabies," said Sarah as she looked between Terry and Paulis.

"I don't think this is an appropriate conversation for adults to have with children at the table," said Vivian.

"Mother, you can't discuss Darwinism without talking about reproduction."

"I guess I'm old-fashioned, but premarital sex is a sin!" She glanced at Roree and Sarah. "You two think you're progressive thinkers and that there's virtue in tolerating every behavior du jour that comes into vogue, except the intolerance of sin. Well I don't tolerate sin. Why can't the progressive thinkers deal with that?"

"Trust me, we tolerate you plenty," said Roree.

The room fell into an awkward silence as everyone focused on their meals.

"Vivian, why don't you tell Terry about the pregnancy case you're working on."

"Roree you know I lost that case." She was so disappointed when that case went to the defense that she had to book a trip Paris. Vivian spent three weeks, drowning her sorrows with French wine and marathon shopping sprees.

"I know, but I thought the kids might find it interesting," said Roree.

Vivian didn't think this topic was appropriate either, but she felt like she was losing the battle. "Well, there was this woman fighting with her insurance company for her sick child with Down syndrome. She knew he was likely to have it before he was born because they did the usual blood tests and amniocentesis.

However, she still decided to keep the child. The insurance company thought an early termination would have proven to be more cost effective. Of course they couldn't force her to have an abortion, but they denied the child's medical bills and everything associated with the Down syndrome as a pre-existing condition. We actually lost the case because the contract she signed was ironclad. It had a eugenics clause backed by the government's new green movement to create healthier children, Lord have mercy!" Vivian wiped her brow with her napkin. "Well, I guess the moral of the story is to keep your DNA and your other private parts to yourself." She caught Terry's eye, "and always read a contract before you sign it."

Terry's phone vibrated and she pulled it from its holster to have a look.

"Honey, we don't do that here," said Sarah.

Paulis, embarrassed, twisted in his seat and slapped his hand to his forehead.

"I'm sorry, it's my mother. She's on her way to pick me up." Terry took another mouthful of the roast and then rose from her seat. "It's been wonderful, meeting everyone."

"I'll help you get your things." Paulis followed her from the table as his family waved goodbye.

Terry's phone vibrated again. "She's here."

"Would you like to invite her in to meet the family?"

Terry frantically waved her finger in the air. "No!"

"Why not?"

"I'll see your forked tongue and raise you three sixes!"

Paulis laughed. "Oh, say no more." Paulis then focused on her luminous lips and leaned in to give her a kiss. Terry received his lips and smiled, lightly touching his cheek as she slid deep into his eyes, feeling something she had never felt before. Then she quickly withdrew and went out to meet her mother. His eyes drifted the length of her tender frame as she left the house.

"Hi, Mom," said Terry as she got into the passenger seat, feeling engulfed by the inviting warmth of the car. Judging by the crisp cobalt blue suit and the hair pulled back tight like Sade Adu's, it was clear that her mother had been shopping with her high society gals today. Her eyebrows were viciously arched beyond reason, creating a sinister, synthetic appeal. Sure, she fronted with Gucci and Tiffany, but the languid posture only made her seem demure. Terry could read her mother like a book.

"So what's his family like? How was dinner?"

She threw her books into the back seat, and looked into her mother's impatient, pinpoint pupils. She could tell her mother was high. The smaller her pupils got, the less reliable her competency as a parent became. "Why, did you want to go in and meet them?" Her mother's sardonic stare mocked and devoured her.

Johanna paused as she considered her daughter's question. She never liked meeting new people while she was relaxed on her medication.

Terry's mother had started using narcotics at a young age after suffering a compound leg fracture during the state gymnastics finals. The injury ended her gymnastics career, but the cravings for pain killers never went away. She became a functional addict.

Johanna got through prep school because they had attentive private tutors there and continuous access to the best prescription drugs and stimulants. Johanna's withdrawal symptoms appeared for the first time when she abruptly quit using during her pregnancy with Terry. This was when her mother realized she had a serious problem. After a long, painful delivery, Johanna was drawn back to the pills.

"You'd better buckle up." said Johanna.

Her mother then eased the gear into drive and maneuvered her way down the road. Terry felt the momentum press her against the heated Coach leather seat as they accelerated. She slid her buckle on, and smiled to herself.

Chapter 11

Vivian was happy to see the evening come to a close, though she was feeling a bit restless. She hadn't received the accolades for her pot roast that she was accustomed to, but judging by the evidence that there were no leftovers, she considered the dinner a success. She turned on the dishwasher, and flicked the light switch off before heading up to the guest bedroom.

She knew Paulis was required to keep his door open during his evening study sessions, so she couldn't resist the urge to slowly walk by his room and take a peek. She entered the room, touching things and looking closely at the shoebox tops on the walls, to see if any of the ones she had recently brought him from Paris were in place. She periodically glanced over his shoulder, impressed with the complexity of the work he was reviewing at this stage in his development. Paulis acknowledged her presence but continued with his computer work, although Vivian continued to linger.

"What's the download Grandma?" He looked up at her inquisitively.

"Paulis, have you seen my earring? I lost one the last time I was here."

"The sapphire and diamond earrings?"

"Yes, they were the one thing your grandfather got right." She smiled.

"No but I'll keep an eye out for it."

"Ok Honey, I'd appreciate that." She continued to hover over him, resisting the urge to touch the holographic images projecting from his monitor. "So, how do you like that new school?"

Paulis exhaled deeply. He knew she had more than a lost earring on her mind. "Dimensions is ok, but it's not what I expected."

Vivian laughed and took a seat behind his chair. "What were you expecting?"

"I don't know. I thought I would be forced to do things. Instead, they really seem to care about us and what we think."

"Well, that sounds ideal. Why didn't you start there when you were in the ninth grade?"

"I was at the top of the waiting list, but they only had room for thirty students."

She considered his response for a moment. "So, you took the place of that poor girl that died?" asked Vivian.

"She didn't die. You know she's in a coma." Vivian waited for him to explain. "Grandma, it was just an unfortunate accident."

"Still in a coma? Well, I guess that poor girl's misfortune was the best thing that could have happened to you."

Paulis thought about her words, and felt angered as a surprising feeling of guilt rose to the surface. He rarely got the point of his grandmother's rants, but he knew they were laced and designed to haunt him when he was old enough to understand. "That's a dark way to look at it. Sometimes, bad things just happen," said Paulis.

"Yes, I'm starting to realize that." She reached for his hand and stroked his finger, noting how the neurotransplant felt like a buffed piece of cartilage.

Paulis snatched his hand away and giggled. "That tickles."

She rolled her eyes. "Honey, you're a marvelous young man, created in God's perfect image, and he has a special purpose for you." Then she gestured at his hand. "This is not God's will."

"How do you know God's will? You have a pacemaker; how is that any different?"

"The pacemaker keeps me alive! I wouldn't have one if I had a choice."

"I know you think that, but you did have a choice, and the option to die seemed absurd considering there was a well-tested, inexpensive pacemaker available!" He began to hyperventilate. "So what you're suggesting is that I need to be sick, before I can benefit from scientific advancement."

Vivian delicately rubbed her chest. "I just think you're being treated like a lab rat, that's all. But that's my opinion, which doesn't seem to count for much around here these days." She reflected a moment, noting that while Paulis's spirit was receptive to change, he was also naïve; that was a dangerous combination. "Honey, don't forget you're only fifteen. I've seen technologies come and go and believe me, the only consistency is that there's always a cost!"

Paulis relaxed and comfortably met her gaze. "My teacher says that whether the changes being made to our bodies and minds, are wise or desirable, misses the crucial point. They are an unavoidable necessity, and intrinsic to the process of taking the human race to the next level." As he spoke these words for the first time he felt empowered, as if he was part of something revolutionary.

Vivian digested his words for a moment. Then she forced her usual hostile smile as an invigorating, protective instinct shifted into place for this hopelessly lost child. "Paulis, at the end of the day, we all have to make the journey on our own. Just don't miss an opportunity to allow wisdom to guide your way."

Paulis spun his chair around, returning his attention to his computer. “Grandma, you just don’t have the capacity to understand like I do.”

Vivian stared at the back of his head in shock, rationalizing his condescending tone to no avail. Then she tucked her bob behind her ear. “Boy you’d better watch your tone.”

He looked back at her, puzzled that she didn’t comprehend his point. “I’m sorry. I didn’t mean to offend you.”

“You don’t have to apologize for having an opinion, but you better be respectful, because you’re not too big for me go upside your head with my pump. Now I understand why you need to wear that protective head gear.”

Paulis smiled awkwardly. “I said I’m sorry.”

“I know, you’re another one of those sorry-ass motherfuckers. I heard you!”

He laughed. “Grandma!”

Vivian laughed. “Ok, I’ll let you slide this time.” Vivian settled back in her chair. “So that Terry seems like a nice girl. She’s smart, pretty, black. She’s perfect.”

“Well, I don’t know about perfect, but I really like her.”

"What do you mean?"

"Terry has the gay gene and the BRCA1 breast cancer gene."

"This just keeps getting better and better," said Vivian sarcastically. "That child's a lesbian?"

"No, just because she has the gene doesn't mean she's going to be gay or have breast cancer."

"Why take the chance?" asked Vivian. "Why do you think those women have the surgery to remove their ovaries and breasts? They don't want to take the chance. Do your parents know about this?"

"No, and I don't want you to tell them, either." Paulis reflected a moment. "So, using technology is ok now? Women removing their breasts and ovaries is ok even though there's a good chance they're perfectly healthy?"

"Don't try to make me look like a hypocrite. There is a difference."

"Look, I like her. She's brilliant and it feels good when she looks at me. Anyway, she says she doesn't feel gay."

"Don't worry I won't say anything." Vivian squeezed her eyes and shook her head knowingly. "Lord, have mercy!"

"What?"

"Didn't they teach you what denial means at that school?"

Roree poked his head in thc door. "Everything ok in here?"

"Yes," said Vivian.

"Vivian, let the boy study."

Vivian smiled to herself, as she walked past Roree to leave the room.

Later that evening, Roree was working in the study and Paulis was in bed with his finger docked in his cell phone, downloading his upcoming lessons. Paulis occasionally glanced at an open book, and some notes that sat beside him.

Sarah was in the bedroom preparing to turn in, but decided to go to the bathroom before the urge struck her. She cautiously moved her body off the bed and made her way towards the bathroom. Suddenly, she caught her silk pajama bottoms on the edge of one of Roree's drawers, which had been left partially open. She thought of how he rarely used this drawer, and how careless it was for him to leave it open. As she went to kick the drawer shut, she noticed a glimmer coming from within. She carefully bent down to open it and found a neat stack of underwear that he no longer wore, and a small zip-lock bag casting a sapphire glow.

Roree hated it when she snooped. She had ruined many a Christmas surprise by allow her eyes to roam where they didn't belong, so she decided to close the drawer and pretend she hadn't seen a thing. She stood up, but her head couldn't let it go. What was he hiding? Was it Vivian's lost earring?

As she moved toward the bathroom, she felt hot shooting pains in her legs. She tried to reach back for the dresser, but her knee twisted inward, and she toppled awkwardly to the floor. She cried out to Roree.

Roree saved his work and came to her rescue, followed by Vivian and Paulis. He glanced at the bottom drawer, before making eye contact with his wife. Then, he noticed the wet spot growing on her pajama bottoms.

Sarah followed Roree's gaze, and realized what was happening.

"Paulis, go on to your room," said Roree.

Paulis just stood there, staring at his mother.

"Paulis!" shouted Roree.

Paulis continued to stand there.

Sarah looked up at him and screamed, "Paulis, get out of here!"

He became angry with frustration as Vivian led him out of the room.

Roree helped her up from the hardwood floor. "I told you to send me a text when you need help. You're gonna break something!"

"My legs felt fine and then they gave out. They're unreliable, so I can't predict when I'll need your help. I'm sorry I've inconvenienced you again." She swiped at the tears falling down her cheeks. "Idiot," she whispered under her breath.

Roree could handle the tears, but it was the puddle of urine that intimidated him. He put a towel on the bed, and sat her down to rest while he went to draw a hot, steamy bath with scented candles and eucalyptus salts.

He helped Sarah into the bathtub and then went to clean up the urine. As he balanced on his knees to scrub the floor and area rug, Roree was startled by a movement in the background. He turned and noticed Vivian watching him. "Can I help you?" asked Roree over his shoulder.

Vivian glared at him, with her mouth turned down. "Maybe you should help yourself and repent while you're down there."

Roree turned from her scrutiny, feeling himself practically gag with the urge to snatch her judgmental eyes from their sockets, but that was not who he was or who he would become. He thought to himself that *he* was not the one who needed to pop a Xanax every time he went to church to receive God's blessings. Then he smiled. "I'll leave the repenting to you and the other saints."

"Coward," Vivian thought to herself. She knew that he was afraid of her, and that deep down, he was just a sniveling little weasel. She also knew that any man who lacked respect for God could not be trusted. Roree was not a crazy man, but the place where his soul resided was sick. Her bitter spit was tempted for his face, but she swallowed instead and left him to scrub the piss from the floor. His place seemed correct for the moment.

Roree put Sarah's soiled clothing in the hamper and sat her cell phone next to the tub. "Call me when you're ready for bed." He kissed her on the forehead.

She was reassured, and finally began to relax as she inhaled the aromatic steam that quietly rose around her. Then her muscles began to throb with pain, and she could barely move. Her body became progressively numb from the waist down, with each minute that passed. Her vision blurred and her cognitive function seemed to fog with the steam that hovered menacingly in the air. She was afraid that the water was too hot, and she just couldn't feel it. She texted Roree in desperation. He saved his work on the computer and ran to see what was going on.

Sarah was sitting in the bathtub crying. "Why is this happening to me?"

He squatted by the tub and rubbed her back, staring at her with his steel blue, emotionless eyes. She used to find his bold stare comforting. It made her feel like he would be the rock if things ever tipped out of control. Now she sensed that he was probably just as numb as her limbs. He was just going through the dutiful motions, and she really had no idea what he was thinking.

Roree put her to bed and then brought her a cup of tea with her evening medications.

Chapter 12

Roree was back at the computer in the study, feeling nauseous from the smell of cleaning products wafting from his hands. His website had sent him a text message, warning of irregular hacking activity. He logged onto the virtual site and saw that thirty members were logged on. Most of them were students in his class, using old cell phones, laptops and tablets which he provided for experimental purposes. Someone had posted a floating banner advertisement on his site that read, "God loves us all, so come join the fold of the righteous." He saw two user names he didn't recognize, chatting with one another. One was named "Godson" and the other "wickedcoolsglchick."

Godson: *"Are you feeling better tonight?"*
wickedcoolsglchick: *"I've been better. I still haven't told my parents."*
Godson: *"Maybe you should."*
wickedcoolsglchick: *"They're just gonna make me get rid of it."*
Godson: *"OMG that's not what God would want! Is that what you want?"*
wickedcoolsglchick: *"No, but they think I'm going to Harvard; I only have one more year left in high school."*

Godson: *"Shouldn't you be in bed by now? It's already after 10:00."*
wickedcoolsglchick: *"It's 1:15 a.m., what city are you in?"*
Godson: *"Los Angeles."*
wickedcoolsglchick: *"Oh, I'm in Boston."*
Godson: *"You should talk to your parents."*
wickedcoolsglchick: *"I've got no one to talk to. I wish I was there with you."*

Roree decoded Godson's encrypted IP address, disabled his outdated antivirus software, and then forced a Trojan virus download onto his smart phone. Within seconds, the user name "Godson" disappeared.

"Idiot," sneered Roree. Then he smiled, catching himself, but not denying the little tingle he felt at the base of his navel. His upload intervention technology was working like a charm.

Roree remained at his computer for an hour, which quickly turned into three. He suddenly became aware of his urge to sleep. His eyes felt like leaky sand bags. He saved his work and shut down the computer, noticing that it was almost 4:30 a.m. After using the bathroom, he removed all of his clothing, except for his underwear, and quietly slipped under the covers next to Sarah. Sarah felt his effort to spoon, and relaxed her muscles to endure him. Roree was trying to figure out how that guy managed to hack into his site to post his religious rhetoric. Feeling a rush of adrenaline in his head, he tucked closer to his wife's warm body.

REM sleep was upon Paulis. He had become accustomed to the beautiful woman's invasion of his unconscious soul. Sleep was supposed to be a place of peace and a time for the soul to evoke dreams of brighter days. Now, intensified by its contrast, Paulis seemed to be trapped in reality even as he slept. Perhaps what happened and how you reacted to it when you dreamed, was just as important as what you did when you were awake. After all, at the end of the day, it was your collective inner peace that kept you levelheaded and rational.

Sarah's upcoming doctor's visit had consumed her thoughts from the time Roree finally came to bed, until she peeled herself away from his collapsed body at 7:30 a.m. She examined her limb's mobility while getting ready for her appointment. Then she moved slowly down the stairs, holding tightly to the handrails. She heard Roree shuffle around in the bedroom, before finally turning on the shower. Vivian was in the kitchen, clearing Paulis's breakfast dishes and preparing coffee. Sarah had regained her strength after last night's bathtub incident, but wondered how long it would be before her legs deceived her again.

Vivian brought Sarah a cup of coffee with her medication and gave her a light shoulder massage. Once they were all ready to go, Roree and Vivian helped Sarah out to the car. Out of the blue, Roree swept her off her feet like a rag doll and gently placed her into the passenger seat. Suddenly, Sarah forgot about the uncertainty she had been feeling, overwhelmed by all the attention and support. On some level, she secretly enjoyed the feeling of being swept off her feet.

"Roree, I can walk, you know?" said Sarah.

"Honey, I know, but I don't want you to fall again." He felt his cell phone vibrate, but ignored it.

Sarah waved to Vivian, as she watched her climb into her car to leave.

"How are you feeling today?" asked Roree, as they pulled into the street behind Vivian.

"I should be asking you. Are you even awake yet? What time did you get to sleep last night?"

"It must have been about 2:00 when I got to bed. I was exhausted, but I got a lot done."

Sarah thought about her mother's words, "Somebody's legs and fix my man!" Why is he lying? Does he even realize he's lying? Sarah heard Roree's cell phone vibrate again, but he continued to focus on the road.

When they arrived at the neurologist's office, Roree double parked and went to lift her out of the car. "Roree, let me walk." She looked at the handicapped ramp, but pointed to the stairs. "I can use the handrails."

Roree's cell phone vibrated again.

"Aren't you going to answer that thing?" asked Sarah.

He paused and then decided to ignore the cell phone, and proceeded to lift Sarah out of the passenger seat. "It's just work. It can wait."

"Roree, stop it; I can use the handrail!"

"Ok," said Roree, clutching her left shoulder and waist from behind, steadying himself with a wide stance.

"Roree get off of me! I know you're in a hurry and you have other things you'd rather be doing, but this isn't about you." She gave him a stern look as she moved away from him, trembling with desperation. "I need to start reconditioning myself. Do you think you could indulge me for five minutes?"

Roree knew the details of his wife's face, as well as he knew his own, so he had ceased to observe them. Now his mind paused abruptly as he focused on what his wife had become, and he dreaded what he might find with his next glance in the mirror. Sarah moved forward, grasping the rail unsteadily with anger and determination. Her legs were familiar to her this morning. Roree released her arm and stood closely behind her. He watched with anxious patience as she ascended to the entrance, occasionally pushing her elbow to reassure her of his presence.

Roree went back to park the car properly, while Sarah waited to be seen by the physician. The officer that was waiting by his car let him slide with just a warning and recommended that he get handicapped parking privileges.

When he returned to the doctor's office carrying Sarah's cane, the receptionist told him that Sarah had already been called into the office. She smiled and subtly pushed her small breasts forward. "Your wife is lucky to have someone so devoted to care for her. I can imagine this must be a major adjustment for both of you."

Roree smiled with pride. "I know I'm not the one that's sick, but it's nice to hear someone acknowledge that it's not easy for the caregiver, either."

Roree took a seat to wait for his wife. He periodically flexed his right hand. His eyelids were heavy, and he was jonesing for another cup of coffee.

After her appointment, Sarah was quiet until they got to the car. "The doctor says I have a urinary tract infection and I'm suffering from depression. He gave me antibiotics and Prozac! He also said I should join one of the MS support groups that Paulis suggested."

Roree focused on the road. "I could have told you that."

Sarah leaned in, never taking her eyes away from his face. "Oh, you noticed?"

"Did he say why you're depressed? You've never suffered from depression before."

Sarah turned her gaze back to the road.

"So what did he say about your MS?" asked Roree.

"He thinks I may be going into remission."

Roree smiled. "That's great news."

She smiled reluctantly, although she knew it would let him off the hook.

---Paulis's Room---

Paulis was home early, seated in front of his computer, surfing the web, but he kept getting pop-ups. He turned his pop-up blocker on and then noticed that his antivirus software had been turned off. Paulis also noticed that his operating system had been running sluggishly, so he ran a full system scan. The scan revealed several medium security Trojan virus intrusions that his system needed to isolate. Paulis approved the virus isolations, and then went to the study to bootup the home's main computer.

The study was dark, illuminated only by the light coming through the glass living room walls. He immediately noticed that the antivirus software was disabled on this computer, as well. Paulis observed Roree's desktop and saw a folder titled, "Virtual

Conditioning." He curiously reviewed the web history, and saw multiple visits to a website with the same name. He tried to access the folder but the system froze whenever he attempted to open it. The files appeared to be protected, but didn't request a password or give an access error.

Paulis felt guilty for trying to invade his father's privacy, but once again, his curiosity got the best of him. How else would he learn what his father was up to? He would certainly grow gray waiting for his father to tell him. Besides, he wouldn't have left the folder in such an obvious place if it was a big secret.

Paulis inserted a USB flash drive and slowly dragged the folder over to its icon. He watched with anticipation as it copied and transferred without a glitch. He opened the trashcan icon and found an older version of the same folder, and dragged it to his USB drive, as well. Paulis smiled to himself as he withdrew the flash drive. He also made a note of the website address before heading back to the privacy of his room. He thought about what his teacher always said. "You must attack a difficult problem from multiple angles, if you're ever to see beyond the cozy confines of your lying eyes."

When he reached his room, he immediately inserted the flash drive into his laptop and launched a program called File Translucent. This program could open just about anything, at the risk of destroying the original data if there was a compatibility issue. If the file contained dangerous or infected data, the program would not discriminate. As a result, Paulis could be exposing his device to significant risk. Paulis wondered if his father was familiar with File Translucent. He was about to find out.

After a few attempts, he finally got the folder to open. The first document he saw was a word document titled “Dimensions Class List.” It contained a list of the thirty students from his class, but his name wasn’t there. He noticed that Terry and four other female students had asterisks next to their names, and their names were on separate folders, within the main folder. He opened Terry’s corresponding folder and found a document with the details of her genetic test results, but nothing else. Then he noticed Shelly’s name was asterisked on the list, and realized that it must have been the student list from the year before he started. Now, he had more questions than answers.

He opened Shelly’s folder and found a PDF file within. It turned out to be a news article about Shelly’s grandfather. He was a wealthy hedge fund manager who met his tragic death in a plane crash two years ago. There was also a photo of Shelly with her father and grandfather, according to the photo caption. The article went on about a multimillion dollar trust her grandfather made available for when she went away to college. Paulis read further about how Shelly created an inexpensive pair of Bluetooth glasses, that added digital depth perception, for those who normally couldn’t perceive it. The article claimed that she was going to be the next Steve Jobs because of her brilliance, and innovative work in creating mobile applications.

Paulis closed Shelly's file, thinking how sad her story had become, now that she was in a coma. He then became angry, wondering why Shelly's story was so important to his father.

Chapter 13

---The Saints---

The sunlight burst into a beautiful array of colors as it passed through the prisms of the church's stained glass windows. Paulis was perplexed as he examined the silver slippers planted firmly on his feet, and the dripping white linen garment that clung to his cold, trembling body. He gazed up at the towering ceiling-length window that restrained and yet supported his weak frame. The cool glass window was soothingly pressed against his cheek, and warmth oozed down his spine. He reached to the right of his back and then to the left trying to find the hole releasing his life blood, but his attempts were in vain. He could hear the gospel choir rejoice behind him so he took a few curious steps backward, struggling to push from the glass wall.

He had already experienced this déjà vu four times. Each time he pushed off the glass wall he relived this backward nightmare as if he were caught in a vindictive, infinite loop.

In a hypnotic trance, he backed into a pool of bloodied holy water. Now baptized and washed of his past, he had a clean slate for what was to come next. His soul drifted in search of it's possibility as he breathed in the surrounding aroma which reminded him of a locker room. He slowly backstroked through the soft water, periodically tasting the iron-rich, chlorine solution, remembering to tuck his palms and scoop the water with each stroke.

He became aware of the preacher's voice. "We are now raised to a newness in life. That if thou shalt confess with thy mouth the Lord Jesus and shalt believe in thine heart that God hath raised him from the dead, thou shalt be saved. On these confessions of your faith I now baptize you in the name of the Father, the Son and the Holy Ghost."

Paulis backed out of the holy pool, continuing his reversed journey in time as the choir began to dig deep with their song:

"Wade in the water,
Wade in the water, children,
Wade in the water,
God's gonna trouble the water."

Whenever Paulis heard this song, he envisioned the haunting stories his grandmother told about the slaves' struggles for freedom. She said it was a song about survival, and part of an important strategy our people used to escape. Water leaves no scent or footprints for those who seek you. During the times of the Underground Railroad, one was not to limit one's self to the mainland. Never leave a trace! The slaves were seduced by the prospects of freedom, and forewarned of the difficult times that would stand in their way. She told him he should be proud of his heritage despite his white father's ancestors who struggled to maintain their stronghold. She said his birth was proof that a blessing could come from centuries of oppression, though the continued dilution of his heritage had been the price. But what price would his children pay, and would it be worth the cost?

Paulis faced the holy pool from which he had just emerged, his body funky with sweat. Surprisingly, the water was clear and inviting, as if he had never bled into it. He continued to step back. Soon he found himself standing next to a line of swaying white robes. Aftershave and biting perfumes whirled between the clapping hands of the Saints. Though he was commingled with the choir, they appeared to know not of his presence. He was a mere spectator as his religious subconscious dominated and had its way.

"This is your invitation to discipleship," said the preacher as the choir echoed cries of joy. Paulis listened and continued his journey backward in time. The blood poured from his back, proof of his crucifixion, as he moved like a slow motion time machine.

He watched the big, charcoaled preacher as he fussed at the congregation. "Jesus died to save our souls from sin. Accept him as your personal savior. The harvest is ripe but the laborers are few, Hallelujah, Hallelujah!! God is calling on you today. He wants to lead you in ways that you never dreamed possible." The breathless preacher wiped the dripping sweat from his brow. "Hallelujah, Hallelujah!"

The gospel choir rejoiced behind the preacher, their cascading robes rocked in synch like dutiful soldiers, set upon their pendulous journey in Christ. However, their hairy demonic tongues vibrated and shivered like a rattlesnake's tail, warning that something wasn't right. Their Gregorian chant echoed out of synch with their rhythmic movements. The sound was beautiful and timeless, but it was not gospel. It was a lie, presented to deceive and contradict. The hairy tongues from which they spoke no longer translated into gospel.

Paulis continued to step backward until he felt a sharp, piercing pain dig and twist into his back. "Ugh," he gasped.

A sexy voice whispered, "Repent from the sins of your flesh."

He moved back, trying to recognize her with the back of his head, but was too afraid to turn and face her. Paulis knew this voice.

Her hand caressed his waistline and her chin landed on his shoulder. Her steamy breath continued, "Who's that girl you're falling in love with? She has a genetic predisposition that's gonna drag you both to Hell." Paulis thought of Terry as he wrestled, with his internal conflict, around all that she was and could become.

The woman placed a heavy gold crucifix in his hands. Paulis stepped back further into the arms of the familiar woman, but found himself standing alone outside the front door of the church. He scanned his warm memories of this place. His back was no longer throbbing with pain, and the warm sounds of the choir were beckoning him from within. The crucifix was gone and he sensed that the nightmare was about to start all over again. It was as if he hadn't just backed his way out of that church, with the blood of Christ pouring from his wound.

His grandmother had always described the church as a place to enjoy fellowship and get gas in her tank. "It was a place to receive the blessings and edifications of the soul," she would say.

He put both of his hands on the door handle and tugged, through his body leaning back, until the huge door gained enough momentum to swing out and welcome him inside. Before he could take a step forward, a big gold crucifix fell from the sky, landing heavily at his feet; its sharp tip digging into the dirt. Paulis struggled to pull it free and then carried it inside.

He soon found himself face to face with the woman. There was nothing between their bodies except the gold crucifix and her strategically placed Texas Instruments. She removed the crucifix from his hands and smiled into his soul. She moved closer until they were nose to nose, delicately rubbing the sharp crucifix across his lower right back. He breathed in, following her rhythm. She sneezed, and bubbles of snot crackled from her ears and nose. When she inhaled, the slime abruptly whistled back in. Paulis quietly hovered under her nose breathing in as she exhaled. With each breath his essence intertwined with hers until he was diminished to a gasp. Each time she inhaled, he suffocated just enough. Then there was a sharp, painful twist and the blood pumped from his back, as she shoved him forward for his spiritual rebirth. Like Jesus, his life would be exchanged for what he was about to become.

He stumbled ahead through the aisles of the church and accepted his invitation for baptism in the holy water. Soon he'd again, be clutched against the church's stained glass window. How long would this cycle continue? When would his transformation be complete? How much more would he have to sacrifice, to prove he was ready?

The church bells rang, and it only took him a moment to realize it was his alarm clock. He eventually awoke with a pillow over his head, breathless and confused as usual.

Chapter 14

Paulis's day had been long. Preoccupied with last night's dream, he was now anxious to get home to study for tomorrow's exams. He decided to stop by the neighborhood Starbucks for an afternoon pick-me-up before heading home. The line that backed up to the entrance of this place at any given hour of the day, never ceased to amaze him. The diversity of people who drank coffee was reflective of the melting pot that Boston had become. He noticed one big bald-headed guy a few people ahead of him texting and laughing to himself with his head down. When the guy looked up, Paulis saw it was his best friend from his old school, but he had changed to the point that he was almost unrecognizable.

"Paulis!" yelled Phillip in surprise.

Paulis was happy to see his old friend. They occasionally texted, but it had been over five months since they had seen each other face to face. His relationship with Phillip was complicated. Phillip was in with the popular crowd, and he would tease Paulis even when others were around, but Paulis knew he meant no harm because he also protected him like a big brother. Paulis never complained about the teasing; still, he wondered when Phillip's empathy would kick in.

They shook hands awkwardly, still in shock to see how much the other had changed. Phillip occasionally stared at the thing covering Paulis's chin, thinking that he looked like a medieval warrior with bad acne. They stood together off to the side, and intermittently texted other people while waiting for their daily fix of caffeine.

"So what's the download, man? How's the new digs?" asked Phillip.

"Dimensions is awesome, but they don't let you get away with shit," said Paulis, trying to sound cool. He noticed that Phillip had put on about twenty-five pounds of muscle since he last saw him at the beginning of the summer.

"Man, that sounds rough. You know I made junior varsity this year?"

"Yes I know. I got your text," said Paulis sarcastically.

"Don't hate! We got a new coach and he's the shit. I'm going for varsity next year, so this year I'm gonna have to go off. I'm just gonna fucking rush!" Paulis watched him explode with excitement, as if he were about to turn into the Incredible Hulk and shred his khakis.

"Let's sit and catch up for a second," said Paulis.

They found an open table and immediately began scarfing down their sweets. Phillip bought three espresso chocolate chunk brownies, and Paulis had white chocolate macadamia nut cookies.

Phillip began picking at a piece of loose trim hanging from the side of the table. Paulis watched his actions, wondering why he was being so destructive. Phillip's reckless behavior made him worry that they might get in trouble, or be asked to leave. It wouldn't have been the first time Phillip caused unnecessary trouble. Paulis thought about how much things had changed since the end of his freshman year, though the undertone was familiar. His best friend seemed to have so much excitement in his life, and Paulis wasn't even sure if his school had competitive sports.

"You know I'm dating Kathy Waterhouse? She's got big tits now and she's a total babe," said Phillip.

"No way!"

Phillip grabbed his crotch, "Way these!"

They both laughed out loud. Their voices blended in with the searing sounds of the cappuccino machines in the background.

"I don't have time to date. All I do now is study."

"Study these!" Phillip made his crotch gesture again. They both laughed uncontrollably. Some of the people around them smiled, and others just rolled their eyes.

Phillip focused on Paulis's finger after catching the reflection off his neurotransplant, and then he stared at the head guard draped across the lower part of his head and neck. "You know there's a rumor that your school is growing armies of babies in the basement of that place?"

Paulis had become accustomed to the neurotransplant as if it were a natural part of him, and for all intents and purposes, it was. The head guard was a beautiful mesh sterling silver work of art, with a groove to hold his Bluetooth. He was proud to wear it. He stroked his smooth fingertip and smiled at Phillip. "Don't be silly."

"So what you're really telling me is that there are no babes at that brain prison you call a school?"

"Let's just say the only thing that's big on those girls is their heads." They both laughed.

"That's rough dude," said Phillip.

"Well, there is one girl that's kind of hot, and she's wicked smart too."

"But?" asked Phillip.

Paulis looked down sheepishly. "Well, I'm just not sure if it's going to work out."

"Who cares if it works out, just put it in!" Phillip sat up and proudly whispered. "Kathy let me feel her up last night."

"No way, I knew I should have stayed at that school! Did she return the favor?"

"No, she was scared. Then her father found out we had the door closed, and he started acting all fatherly and shit."

"Well you'll get no sympathy from me."

"I thought I told you not to hate; Bitch!"

Paulis grabbed his crotch. "Hate these!"

Once again they both burst out in adolescent laughter, holding their stomachs. Paulis missed the world where aimless laughter like this carried no consequences. His new reality was consumed with tight schedules, where every action carried a calculated work to reward outcome. Being a carefree child did not carry the cachet it did a year ago. Had he known his life was about to change so drastically, he would have appreciated it more, but there wasn't enough money in the world to make him go back. It was like the next layer of his life was being put into place, and to unravel it now would be like trying to peel away a layer of his skin. He was still awkward and fumbling at every turn, but the power surging from his core was steady and focused, so now he had what was most important. He had clarity.

"So why have you stopped hanging out with us? Are you too good for us now?"

Paulis put his nose in the air. "Oh, don't be so obtuse!"

"Obtuse these," said Phillip.

Paulis smiled, but his disposition had become more serious. "Actually, I miss hanging out with you guys. I'm a little stressed out with all the pressures from school."

"Paulis, you're already smart. Why are you stressed?"

"They're all smarter than me, and I'm having strange dreams almost every night. I even punched my father once when he woke me up." Paulis was breathing rapidly.

Phillip watched him, amused, hoping Paulis wasn't about to start crying right there in public and embarrass him, as he had done in the past.

"Wet dreams?" asked Phillip, before stuffing half a brownie into his mouth.

"Not exactly, but there is a naked woman."

"Is she fucking with your freaky toes?" mumbled Phillip through the rotating chocolate mass in his mouth.

Paulis hadn't thought about his missing toes in some time. "No, and fuck you, by the way! It's like she knows what I'm afraid of, and she uses that information to threaten me."

"You're dreaming about some naked, blackmailing psycho bitch? That's some weird, freaky shit, my four-toed friend."

"Why are you so obsessed with my toes?"

"I'm not obsessed, but the people at school were asking about you. They asked, where did Foe Toe go?" Phillip burst into laughter.

Paulis tried to laugh and be a good sport as usual, but he no longer had the desire to be patient with this type of behavior. He never had to put up with this level of ignorance and immaturity at his new school. They both took awkward sips from their coffees and fiddled with their phones, checking their text messages.

"So, how's your mother doing?" asked Phillip, without looking up from his phone.

"She's better, but still weak. She fell the other day."

"Do you know how long she has to live?"

"She's not dying, but her MS symptoms will come and go. Sometimes her legs are paralyzed."

"Is she in a wheelchair?"

"No, but she has a cane to keep from falling."

"How can she be paralyzed and not be in a wheelchair?"

"She's not always paralyzed."

"I've never heard of that," said Phillip in frustration. They both fell silent, and Phillip went back to yanking at the lose trim on the table.

"I'm getting a letterman jacket this year. You should come to watch us play for the homecoming game. You should see our offensive line; it's fucking sick! We're going to have beer afterwards."

Paulis rolled his eyes. "You know I don't drink and where are you guys gonna get beer?"

"Oh, come on, don't be such a freak! You're in high school now. Who the hell cares where it comes from?"

"I believe the legal drinking age was twenty-one, last time I checked."

Phillip laughed. "So? Why don't you ask your parents if they drank before they were twenty-one?"

"No doubt, but they didn't have an IQ of 140."

"Paulis, you can't go around telling people your IQ. That shit's lame."

Paulis grabbed his crotch. "Lame these. So, how's your father doing?"

Phillip looked him dead on and flicked at the swaying trim hanging from the table, "Drinking like a fucking fish; you're lucky your father is there for you."

He could now see the Phillip he remembered from last year, slightly uncertain of himself, yet on the verge of finding his way. Paulis thought about how little he saw his own father and how little they interacted when he was around. Suddenly, he felt like an imposter. "Yes, I guess I am lucky that he takes good care of us, especially with all that's been happening with my mother. You can always come by and hang with me, if you ever need to escape for a bit."

"Ok, thanks." Phillip thought to himself that this was an empty gesture, and he probably wouldn't see Paulis again for several months. Paulis was becoming an old snob and had too many problems to count. He didn't even have a girlfriend yet.

Phillip continued to stare at Paulis's mesh head guard with amusement. Paulis stared back at him suspiciously, daring him to ask about it.

Chapter 15

Paulis's clock read 3:07 a.m., Friday morning. The events of the day had streamed nonstop through his mind, ruining his ability to relax. His charged dreams, one more dark and stimulating than the other, dominated, and shifted all that was not secured into place. School was supposed to be a safe haven, but his studies had not progressed the previous afternoon, so he felt anxious, and now questioned his capabilities. He was also unsettled by the earlier interaction he had with his friend at Starbucks. The exposure he felt when in situations ungoverned by the rules and protection of Dimensions was nerve-rattling, so the fact that he was having problems sleeping was of no surprise. When he was a child, his mother used to give him warm milk to help him sleep. It had worked in the past, so he decided to head to the kitchen and give it a try.

He felt his way through the darkness of the upstairs hallway, but noticed a glow illuminating the borders of the door to the study. Paulis carefully crept to the door and listened as he watched the shades of light dart through the seams. He pressed his ear to the door and heard the quickened clicking of a keyboard. He hesitated to open the door for fear of what he might find, but his curiosity would not be denied. Paulis cracked the door open and peeked inside. The glow of the holographic monitors paralyzed him with apprehension. His attention was then drawn to the back of his father's head which feverishly bobbed between the two computer monitors. Paulis swallowed hard, but his mouth was pasty and stale, which made it difficult to clear his throat. Here in the dark confines of the night, he watched his father, knee-deep in what might be his family's greatest shame.

"What are you doing?" asked Paulis.

"Paulis, go back to bed," replied Roree, without turning around.

Paulis stared at the familiar fingerprint-protected screenshots of the school's website on one screen, and on the other, his father was launched in the middle of a live chat with someone.

"That's ok; I already know what you're doing," said Paulis, in an accusatory manner.

Roree minimized all of the open screens and spun his chair around to meet his son's roaming eyes. "What's that Paulis; what am I doing?"

Paulis saw an unfamiliar glazed look on his father's face and suddenly regretted having entered the study. "You're hacking into the school's website, and I know all about that website you're building. You're gonna get me into trouble with the school, if you get caught."

"My project has nothing to do with your school. Why were you going through my things, anyway?"

“I just saw you in a restricted area of the school’s website that’s designated only for the students. Do you think that I’m stupid or something?”

“I’m not logged onto the site. Those are just screenshots of what the site looks like. I’m in the process of making suggestions for updates,” said Roree.

Paulis frowned. “You didn’t think I could get into Dimensions on my own, did you?”

“Well, you certainly didn’t get in the first year, but that’s neither here nor there. The point is, you got in.” Roree’s bold gaze penetrated through him.

Paulis looked down to avoid his stare, and flexed his deformed bare toes. “I guess you don’t have any confidence in me?”

Roree followed Paulis’s gaze to his feet. “It’s you that needs to have confidence in yourself, and I’m gonna need you to take that to heart. Speculating about what others may or may not think can be a dangerous game.”

Paulis hated it when adults evaded his questions. He felt like it was a subtle dishonesty and cowardice. “What do you know about Shelly’s grandfather?” asked Paulis.

“I don’t know anything about Shelly, except that she’s in a coma. Why are you still up? Don’t you have an exam in the morning?” Roree’s voice was controlled as he cringed, suppressing his hatred toward the man who bamboozled his father out of his fortune. Paulis would never understand the lengths he had taken, to exact revenge on Shelly's family for ruining their lives. He was too innocent to accept the deeds that needed to be done to enable his advancement. There were some things that his son didn't need to know.

Paulis didn't want to believe that his father had intentionally harmed Shelly for his benefit, but Dimensions had taught him to see that which was before him, even when it was ugly. Paulis didn't know what his father's motivation was. He never thought about that before. He only knew that the files he took from his father's computer just weren't right.

"Yes, my exam is at 8:00 a.m. I just can't sleep," said Paulis.

"You want to talk about it?"

Paulis stared at his father inquisitively. He had already tried to discuss his problems with Phillip the day before, and was not about to make that mistake again. "Why do you care all of sudden?"

"Of course I care. I wouldn't have asked if I didn't care. Are you intentionally trying to be offensive?" asked Roree.

"It's just that you never spend time with me. You're rarely home, and when you are, you're hiding in here."

“First of all, nobody’s hiding, so I think you need to stop projecting. I’m in here taking care of business. You have no idea what it’s like to be a grown man. You need to be in full command of everything or you’re perceived as weak. You’ll understand, once you have a family of your own.”

Paulis looked at his father, noting that he was in control, and though he wished he had more time with him, he couldn’t deny that his father was working to make his life better. “I think I understand,” said Paulis.

“Good. I’m happy to hear it. So, have you found another girlfriend yet?”

“Terry’s my girlfriend,” said Paulis. He was starting to feel foolish trying to figure out if his father was upset or just toying with him.

Roree studied him intently for a moment. “I thought she was undecided about men?”

“How would you know about that? I’ve never mentioned anything about her genetic testing!”

“Who said anything about genetic testing? It’s obvious by the way she carries herself. Apparently her mother is no prize, either. Your mother met her for lunch the other day.”

“You’re just a liar pretending like you give a fuck. I hate that I’m stuck with you as my father. You’re a shitty excuse for a human being!" Paulis breathed heavily, but held back his tears.

"Who do you think you're talking to? You're starting to sound like your grandmother, except you wouldn't catch her crying like a little girl."

Paulis's mouth parted, dry with desperation.

Roree leaned forward in his chair as if to whisper a secret, "Paulis you need to get a grip." His voice remained low but shaky as he scrutinized his son. "Now go back to bed and let me finish my work."

Paulis shrank into the shadow of the computer monitor's glow, then turned and left the study.

"Paulis, get the door."

Paulis went back and slammed the door. He then leaned with his back against it, easing his heavy heart as it pumped with adrenaline. He regretted the horrible things he had said. He wished he could delete the last five minutes of his life, or better still, his entire life. He decided to wait for his father to comfort him, like he had done in the past, when he was upset.

On the other side of the door, Roree wondered how much Paulis had figured out about his work. In his mind he retraced the trail of documents he kept on his computer as his anger momentarily flared. This was not the first time Paulis had declared his hatred toward him.

Roree was a little relieved to see Paulis exert himself, even if it was encased in an emotional fit.

What if his son really knew what he was up to? What if the hate was real this time? He loved Paulis, but he wasn't going to provide him with so much comfort and warmth that it stifled his journey into manhood.

Roree's heart sank as his conscience got the best of him; after all, Paulis was still only fifteen. Just as he saved his work and got out of his seat to go talk to him, the computer beeped. He checked the screen and saw that "Godson," the guy who previously hacked his website, had logged on. Roree sneered, and bounced back down into his chair.

Paulis waited in the dimly lit hallway as his heartbeat slowly returning to a normal pace. Then he heard the familiar clicking of the keyboard, while his mind spewed a nebulous sense of dread. It was at that pivotal moment that he realized his greatest fear. He was on his own.

Chapter 16

The Dimensions cafeteria caught no sunlight but the ceiling, rising ten stories above, gave it boundless possibilities to create a potential energy of its own. Terry watched Paulis from across the lunchroom table. He hadn't looked her way in almost five minutes; he usually couldn't take his eyes off of her. He was the last one to leave class, so she was wondering how he did on the exam. She observed how his delicately waxed brown dreadlocks and thick, bushy eyebrows accentuated the face of a little boy. Yet, the congealed frown of his brow bolstered restrained worry and discontent.

He was a stranger to her and so far away. So why was she falling in love with him? She knew she would never accompany him on the voyage deep inside his head. Perhaps he decided, long ago, that the risk of her becoming a lesbian was too great. Her genetic predisposition had placed limitations on how much he would be able to give of himself. She speculated that anytime he spent beyond those limits would be a source of anxiety for him. So, why did she expect him to be different from anyone else? She was a beautiful black canvas, expecting profound works and endless possibilities from her life. The limitations of others would never influence who she was or who God designed her to become. Her vulnerability was associated with the fact that her heart continued to beat independent of all logic. If her grandmother had taught her anything, it was that this weakness could be controlled, too.

Paulis yawned and rubbed his tired eyes. He noticed Terry checking him out, and wondered how long he had been consumed in his daydream. “What are you staring at?”

Terry noted how the bags under his eyes made him look exhausted and worn down. “Just wondering what you’re thinking.”

“Is life all about money?”

She straightened her silk Burberry scarf and laughed. “Pretty much,” she said, then her demeanor changed. “How did the exam go?”

Paulis’s chin dipped. “I didn’t sleep well last night.”

“Is that an excuse for something?”

He wanted to tell her that he had been strapped to his bed for most of the night, teetering between the fine line of ecstasy and torture. However, he decided that she probably didn’t share his views on the plausibility of such an event. “Have you ever felt like being awake is just one aspect of reality?”

Terry delicately bit her lip and batted her eyes. “What do you mean?”

"How would you feel if you could get away with doing something while you were awake, but then suffered the consequences when you went to sleep?"

"That sounds like guilt." She placed her finger on his temple resisting the urge to brush the crumbs from his cheek, because this was not the time for that. "It's all in your head."

"That, among other things," he laughed briefly before settling back. "But does that make it any less relevant, and is the punishment any less severe than if you were awake?"

Terry contemplated his question, which both annoyed and challenged her. "I don't know, Paulis, you tell me. How severe was it?"

He sat up and crossed his arms. "I knew you wouldn't understand."

She impatiently swept her hand through her hair. "Perhaps you're not making any sense."

He took a deep breath while rehearsing his story, fighting his instinct to hold back. "I've been having these recurring images of a woman coming to me in my dreams. I know she's a subconscious manifestation of something, but it's like she has this power over me."

Terry watched him intently.

"She tells me what I should be doing when I'm awake and if I don't do it she punishes me when I'm sleeping."

She laughed. "You sound like my uncle when he would smoke marijuana," said Terry.

"You know I don't smoke weed and where the hell would I get some weed, anyway?" He breathed rapidly.

"I don't like that aggressive tone, and I didn't say you were getting high. I was simply suggesting that you sound like you've been getting stoned out of your fucking mind! That's all." She batted her eyes innocently and forced a smile. "I was just kidding. What's the download with you?"

Paulis stared at her blankly. Then, he took her hand and closed his eyes as he gently rubbed his neurotransplant against hers.

"If I could somehow touch my thoughts to yours, you would see how confused I am about my feelings for you." He reviewed his words and began to deeply regret them.

Terry noted the tremulous innocence in his voice and immediately began to forgive him for what he was about to do. She pulled her hand away, so he couldn't feel her stiffen with fear. "Paulis, why are we having this ridiculous conversation? What's wrong?"

"It's just not good for me to be hanging out with you right now," he said, sighing with relief.

She mumbled angrily to herself. "Touch your thoughts with mine; next time, just send me a text!" Then the sting of his words caught her off guard, and the tears rolled down her cheeks. "I'm gonna tell!"

She got up and stormed away, leaving him alone to finish his lunch.

---Metropolis Saüc Restaurant---

Sarah adored the Metropolis Saüc. The atmosphere reminded her of a small NYC restaurant without pretensions. The ambience was intimate yet energetic, stylish but unfussy and the chicken soup was to die for.

Sarah had been waiting twenty minutes for Johanna, Terry's mother, after having received her text message saying it was urgent that they meet. Her muscles were feeling funny today, so she was worried that her MS could be coming out of remission. She felt self-conscious about carrying a cane around at her age. She was aware of the pity and inquisitive looks she got from people, but she could deal with that. It was the individuals who looked right through her that robbed her of her essence. Then again, maybe she was the one who stared, wondering if her growing hostility had yet to register on her face.

“Hello, Sarah,” said Johanna.

Sarah initially focused on Johanna’s familiar face, but immediately froze when she saw Dr. Jones was with her. She hadn’t spoken to Dr. Jones since her discharge from the hospital. The same day Dr. Jones nonchalantly told her she might be adopted.

“Dr. Jones, what are you doing here?”

“Well hello to you, too,” said Dr. Jones. “Why wouldn’t I be here?”

Sarah looked at Johanna. “What is she doing here?”

“I thought you knew I’m on the board of directors for Dimensions. My interest in this matter is just as real as yours,” said Dr. Jones. They both took seats at the table.

“We’re here to discuss the children, not the school,” said Sarah.

“The children and the school are one in the same, don’t you think?” replied Johanna, as she tugged at her nose.

“And besides, Terry’s my granddaughter,” said Dr. Jones proudly, focused on Sarah.

Sarah’s eyes widened as she looked from Johanna to Dr. Jones and back, noting how the light ruthlessly revealed the caked on layers of foundation Dr. Jones used to disguise her years of wisdom. "She's your mother?"

"Yes," said Johanna as she lightly rubbed her nose. "How do you two know each other?"

"You didn't know she was my doctor?" asked Sarah, as she searched Johanna's smooth, bronzed face and chiseled bone structure, trying to gauge her level of sincerity.

"Sarah was my patient," said Babette to Johanna. Then she went back to Sarah. "I've always maintained strict confidentiality, but now that our relationship has changed, I guess you can start calling me Babette."

Sarah was a little relieved that Dr. Jones, or now Babette, claimed to maintain her professional decorum, but the situation still felt strange. It seemed that every time she encountered Dr. Jones, her life got turned inside out.

"Well, if we're done with the introductions, I'd like to discuss the children," said Johanna.

"Ok, so what's up?" asked Sarah. She ignored the energy from Babette's burning stare in her periphery.

"Terry blogged that they broke up this afternoon," said Johanna.

"Oh, I didn't realize that."

"We need you to talk to your son and get him back on track," said Babette.

"On track?"

"Yes, apparently he's been acting like something's wrong. Did he fail his exam this morning? Is he sleeping ok?" asked Johanna as she sniffled and lightly touched her nose.

Sarah was a little taken aback. "I doubt that he failed any exam, but he has been a little distant. My husband noticed it, too."

"Well, you should speak with him," said Johanna. "We need them to be together throughout this process."

The ladies were quiet for a moment and finally Babette perked up and tossed her long shiny hair. Sarah followed Babette's eyes to the waiter as he approached their table.

"What can I get for you young ladies?" asked the waiter.

"Young? This is my daughter," laughed, Babette.

"Oh, I thought you were sisters," he quipped.

Johanna rolled her eyes and gave the waiter her order.

Babette flirted with the waiter like a horny college girl as she inquired about the vegan menu. The waiter, who was clearly gay, flirted back. She boldly basked in his gaze until he finally sashayed away with their orders. Babette hated that her beauty held no power over gay men. If anything, their sharp tongues had been a source of piercing anxiety because they saw right through her, that is, unless she was dressed flawlessly.

Babette discovered her feminine wiles at an early age. She had found herself entwined with some of the older boys in the neighborhood and became pregnant when she was only thirteen. She tried to keep it a secret for as long as she could, but the shame had eaten away at her.

One day, she came home early from school with an upset stomach and ran into the landlord, who was flushed and tucking his shirt into his pants, as he left her home. Babette had suspected that her mother was having men over when her father was away, but now she had proof. Of course, she was more worried about the new life she had growing inside her belly. Her mother told her that thirteen was too young to be a mother, and her father would be very disappointed that the apple of his eye was spreading her legs for the entire neighborhood to see. Her mother also said that life was all about second chances, and with a little trust, this situation could be turned into a bonding experience.

Her mother scraped the fetus from her uterus that very afternoon. By the time the bleeding finally stopped, Babette was convinced that the events of that day brought the two of them closer. Her mother promised to keep their little secret as long as she didn't tell her father about what she thought she saw.

A year later, her mother took her own life. At first, she mourned the loss of the closest person in her world. Then she grew to realize that her mother had betrayed her, and that bringing her close was merely a tool she used to break her down. Everything that she thought was real had vanished just when she needed it the most. Once she finally figured out the score, she put her head down and ran for her life. She began to resent her father for not protecting her. But on some level she knew it wasn't his fault. He just wasn't ready to maneuver through the minefield he unlocked when he slipped the wedding band on her mother's pointing finger.

The ladies dined in the silence brought on by a delectable cuisine that consumed, and demanded nothing less. Throughout their meal, Sarah observed the twisted interaction between the waiter and Babette with amusement. She pitied any man who got snagged between this woman's deadly thighs; however, she had to admire the waiter, who skillfully earned his tip.

Sarah blew into the steam of her coffee to cool it down before she took a sip. "So, is Terry gay?"

Johanna rolled her eyes and looked in Babette's direction.

"Gay or straight has nothing to do with the functionality of her ovaries and uterus, you know that," said Babette as she flashed her tall, bleached teeth and reapplied her aristocratic red lipstick.

Sarah was having trouble processing Babette's remarks. It reminded her of something she might say just for effect, but now it stirred up a mixture of emotions. Had Paulis made a mistake that he corrected, by breaking up with Terry? Clearly, she would have to speak with him later that night to get a straight answer. Sarah was a traditional mother and she wanted grandchildren because she believed in a strong family. She had never gotten over growing up without her father. Of course, if things went as planned she would have grandchildren, but there would be nothing traditional about it. It was true that Terry's uterus and ovaries functioned independent of her will or desire to have children, but this situation was more complicated than mere human anatomy. Paulis would have to decide if he wanted Terry and everything that came along with her. It was his decision, and she would not interfere.

"So, how's the vaccine coming along?" asked Babette. She and Johanna intently awaited her response.

"It should be ready to try out on the seniors by graduation," said Sarah.

"That's great!" said Johanna. "Are there any little worries to share?"

"The company supplying me with the neurotransplant-prepped rats is behind in their production. I should have the order by the end of the month, certainly within time to test the vaccine for safety. After the kids receive the inoculation download of the vaccine, their offspring will have the same neurological changes that they currently possess. Their offspring will also inherit all of the downloaded information they've acquired and maintained in their long-term memory."

Babette smiled proudly and took a sip from her virgin daiquiri. "Outstanding!"

Chapter 17

---GABA Rap---

Terry sighed with relief as she pulled around the circular drive in her father's BMW ActiveHybrid. After her sixteenth birthday she took possession of the car, since it was just collecting dust while he was away on one of his many business trips. One day, she would pull up in her own car, to her own home, and hopefully have someone to share it with.

She scrutinized the big, white Tuscan pillars that framed the building's classical architecture, a theme that continued as she entered the home. If she ended up all alone, she thought there certainly wouldn't be a need for anything extravagant like this.

Johanna and Babette greeted her as soon as she opened the door. She felt like she had walked into an intervention as they descended upon her. "We love you," said her mother as she gave her a big hug. "So, you want to tell us what happened?"

"You want to wait until I get my jacket off?"

They watched her remove her backpack and jacket, placing them on the table. She looked like she wanted to cry.

“You’re not having sex, are you?” asked her grandmother with concern, as she freed a strand of hair from Terry’s head guard.

A small part of Johanna got excited, hoping that Terry’s feminine instincts had kicked in, and her desire for men had become so overwhelming that she could no longer control herself. Then she suppressed her reckless thoughts, because she knew Terry was not ready for sex.

“Of course not,” said Terry, noting that Babette hadn’t given her a hug.

“Good. Getting pregnant before you get the vaccine would be tragic,” said Johanna.

“Then I don’t understand why you’re so upset over Paulis. Can’t you choose someone else?” asked Babette.

“Because I love him,” cried Terry.

“Oh that,” said Babette as she rolled her eyes. “At your age, maybe you just have indigestion. I’ve seen what they pass off as food in that cafeteria.”

Babette never understood the concept of love. She thought it was mere sugar coating for more primitive impulses. Sure, she believed in feeling deeply for someone and that you should look out for the people you cared about and trusted. However, she also believed that when things changed, you needed to let go and move on. Things always changed.

“Have you ever loved anyone, Grandmother?” asked Terry, as she held back her tears.

Babette remembered having the same question when she was sixteen, but she never received adequate answers. Love had twice stripped her of her dignity, and blinded her to realities she would have otherwise seen right before her eyes. She had vowed to never be caught off guard, again.

“You know I can’t answer that,” said Babette. “I’m not even sure I understand what that means. I just hate to see you get so worked up over this.”

“How could someone as old as you not know what love is?” Terry always regretted when her first thought leaped out of her mouth. She knew to never call a woman old, even if she was.

Surprisingly, Babette didn’t seem to react to the statement. Then again, she rarely reacted. If anything, she probably thrived on the raw, unedited data. Still, Terry didn’t understand how Babette couldn’t love her. She just didn’t see the emotional risk Babette took on by loving her own granddaughter.

Babette delicately considered Terry’s question. “I guess I’ve had a long time to think about it, and I question its usefulness. But I feel something different for you, and it’s because you’re special. It has nothing to do with family obligations, nor does it come with any conditions of duration. It’s now, and I don’t feel the need to further define it.”

Johanna couldn't believe Babette would not just lie and say she loved Terry, knowing the child had just been dumped by her boyfriend. She knew from a lifetime of experience that her mother genuinely had no idea what love was, and the more Babette analyzed it, the less she cared for it. Johanna also understood Babette's, limits so context was important when Johanna found herself starting to judge. She just wished she could protect her daughter from her grandmother's insensitivity.

"We have something for you," said Johanna, as she motioned for Terry to move toward the formal dining room.

As they entered the room her eyes immediately zoomed in onto the big white box and extra widescreen tablet that was placed on the long, mahogany dining table. She quickly opened the box. She loved surprises, but soon became perplexed as she peered inside. "What is it, a hair dryer so I can look nice and girly?" asked Terry, as she sarcastically batted her eyes at her mother.

"No, your father left them for you," said Johanna.

"Oh, what is it?" asked Terry as she carefully pulled a black dome out of the box. Since it was from her father, she knew it had to be special. She struggled to hold it up to the lights of the crystal chandelier as she gazed into the center of its wiry matrix.

"It's called GABA Rap. There's another one over here," said Johanna, as she pulled an identical box from under the table. She opened it and clamped the black dome to the back of the chair and leaned against it as it threatened to topple over. "We also have the software to make it work. Your grandmother and I thought maybe it would help take your mind off things."

"What's it for?"

"They're like portable MRI machines, but they've been altered to allow people to share past thoughts," said Babette.

Terry was thunderstruck with excitement but quickly became fearful as the gravity of what her grandmother was suggesting sank in. "That seems like a lot of work. Can't you just tell me what you want me to know about your past? I mean, does it actually work?"

"I would think my willingness to share uninterrupted thoughts with you would create a level of trust, unduplicated by mere conscious dialogue. You would be able to learn about history; my history."

"I'm only interested in what you're thinking now, and you can tell me that yourself."

"You should show a little more respect for history," said Babette as she clamped the other dome to the adjacent chair. "Take a seat." She quickly moved around the table, plugging the two domes into the large tablet, and switched on the power.

She stared at the domes and the big, colorful tablet's screen with curiosity, wondering why the connections between the domes and the tablet were not wireless. "History can't tell me anything about how you feel right now," said Terry.

"No, but it can give you emotional context, and that's certainly not something you can read or download from a book."

"If you love me, can't you just say it?"

Babette shook her head and pointed to the chair. "Child, this is not about love. I want you to see that it's possible to rise above it all. I also want you to think about the big picture, and the implications that GABA Rap could have on the world."

Terry looked at her grandmother, shocked that this was something she was planning to dole out to everyone. She began to see that this process was not about her. Dimensions, this new GABA Rap, the vaccine that would allow her to pass her knowledge on to her offspring, were all part of a bigger plan to change the trajectory of society as we knew it. She realized she was on the ground floor of exciting and disruptive technology, but it had nothing to do with her. It wasn't about being an individual. The sooner she accepted that, the better she would understand her role. There would be many rewards for sacrificing her future to the unknown. She was honored, and she was ready.

Terry removed her sterling silver head guard and placed it on the table. She sat in the chair and pulled the dome over her head. "It's a little uncomfortable on my head."

"Yes, I know. We were hoping you could do something to make it more user-friendly and comfortable," said Babette. Babette removed Terry's head guard from the table and put it in the kitchen, before returning to take a seat under the second dome. "You ready to try it?"

Terry took a deep breath and gulped down a mouthful of air before giving her the thumbs up. Johanna had pensively drifted into the background, and watched in fear while resisting the urge to cover her eyes.

"Ok, keep your eyes closed until we're done." said Babette, as she pushed the start button on the tablet.

At first, all Terry saw was darkness, as the dome rested uncomfortably on her head. Then, she saw an image of what appeared to be a younger Babette. She was standing with a muscular bad boy who wore a dingy wife-beater. The boy had bloody nail marks on his cheek and breathed heavily, as if he had recently been in a fight. He hooked his tattooed arm around Babette's slender waist, whispering to her to keep quiet as an ambulance with flashing lights blurred in the distance.

"What have you done? Maxine is my best friend!" She cried and shivered against him.

The boy pulled her close and shushed her, not allowing her to escape his gaze. He then placed his full black lips on top of hers, covering her entire mouth. The young Babette's posture steadied into his embrace as she stared, entranced by his bold moves. She slowly ran her hands upward, caressing his chiseled biceps, until reaching his broad shoulders with a sigh. The image faded away.

Terry immediately pushed the dome off of her head and looked straight across the table at Babette. "Who was that guy you were with?" asked Terry with concern.

Johanna looked at Babette and rolled her eyes, wondering which sexual exploit her daughter had just witnessed.

"I don't know who you saw and I'm not interested. I'm just going trust you with it," said Babette.

"But what am I supposed to do with it? I've never seen you cry before. Why would you want me to see that?"

"Perhaps I've misjudged you. I thought you could handle it."

"I can handle it, but that's not the point."

"Then what's the point?"

“What if I couldn’t handle it? What if I saw something my brain couldn’t handle?” Terry asked, breathing heavily.

“Your brain would probably suppress it until you were mature enough to process it, just like it does with any other traumatic event. This is one of the reasons your father’s company wasn’t able to get FDA approval.”

“Will the suppressed traumatic events be passed on to my offspring with everything else, after I am vaccinated?”

“Theoretically, yes. That’s why we need you to tweak the software with a few safeguards and put limitations on what gets transferred.”

Terry had attended the junior code hacker’s summer camp for two summers in a row. Tweaking the program that came with these outdated MRI machines would be a breeze. She took a deep breath and began formulating ideas on how to make GABA Rap safer.

“Now, tell me what *you* saw?” asked Terry.

Babette had seen Terry’s thoughts about Paulis, and her dreams of them being together with their own children in a big home. But the children came with flashing images of wheelchairs, and deformed heads so big that they toppled over. She was conflicted about her sexuality and was afraid that she would never find a mate, now that Paulis had rejected her.

"I saw how you really do care about Paulis, and that you miss your father." Babette glanced briefly at Johanna.

Terry thought to herself how her grandmother was right. While she loved Paulis, she missed her father most of all. Whenever he was in town, he showered her with attention and gifts. He was always amazed at how bright she was. When he was away, her mother completed her motherly duties as expected, but she never seemed to be all there. Her mother recited "I love you" daily, but there was something empty about it. Johanna didn't seem to have a handle on her own life, so how was she supposed to guide her daughter's as well?

On the other hand, Babette never expressed love, but Terry could sense that she was in charge of her life, and would move heaven and earth for her. Terry took great comfort in this, and felt like no matter what difficulty she expressed, Babette would have her back. Sadly, with her mother, if her needs became too complicated, she suspected the love would dwindle. Her suspicions were confirmed when Terry got her genetic test results back. While the gay gene had thrown her mother for a loop, it was the positive BRCA1 breast cancer gene that shook her mother to bits, because it required her to take action and get tested. Johanna's positive test results brought an unspoken resentment to the surface.

If Terry hadn't felt responsible for her own well-being before, she certainly felt it then. She knew that

Johanna found no value in learning about potential problems. All she saw was something new to worry about and another reason to get high. Terry dealt with her own uncertainty, just as she always suspected she would have to. Then she dealt with her mother's truth.

"How are your sinuses today?" asked Terry, as she watched her mother sniffle and rub her nose.

Johanna studied her daughter's face, stunned by her cruelty. Terry had figured out that there was no sinus problem by the time she was ten. Sinus problems had become the unspoken code for narcotic addiction.

"Have you ever thought of trying rehabilitation?" asked Terry.

"It's under control, so don't you worry about it."

Babette gently took hold of Johanna's arm. "Well, if you ever feel that rehab is necessary, we're always here to support you."

Johanna sneered at Babette for undermining her authority, as she pulled her arm away. Babette was acting out the "concerned parent, who happened to be a physician," playbook. However, the reality was Babette had written many prescriptions for her over the years so she was being a bit of a hypocrite.

Terry stared at her, wondering if she was really this limited, or if there was a hidden dimension her mother possessed. Everybody had something special. She refused to believe the "what you see is what you get," image that Johanna shamelessly pushed forward.

"Would you like to try GABA Rap with me?" asked Terry.

"No thanks. I'll wait until you've ironed out all of the kinks." Johanna was not interested in sharing her thoughts through this contraption. She believed in the old saying, "it's better to be thought a fool, than to speak and remove all doubt."

Johanna's lifetime of failures and disappointments stood on their own, but the shame that accompanied those short-comings was hers alone. Nobody would ever be able to judge her for her true feelings of insecurity; they could only speculate.

Chapter 18

The branches clawed at the trembling windows, blurring the perception between what nature intended and that which seeped between the fragile seams woven by man.

Roree logged off the computer and felt a momentary guilt flush over him as he watched the screens go dark. His feelings of guilt were interspersed with his obsessive need for perfection in his work. It was 3:30 when he finally slid into bed, exhausted, and clung to his wife's body. Sarah intertwined her lower legs with his and pulled him close.

Just down the hall, Paulis desperately clung to his pillow as he shifted uncomfortably in bed. He felt as if he had been drugged because he was so tired, but still, he couldn't get to sleep. His level of consciousness had become blurred, and the only thing he knew for sure was that his thoughts were not to be trusted.

He had forgotten to turn the lights off, so when they flickered, the sound in his ears went in and out. His eyes scanned the ceiling and focused on a tiny spider that moved slowly toward the light. The shoebox tops on the bedroom walls seemed to have merged into a big, colorful mural, making him dizzy. He squeezed his dry, tired eyelids together. He could feel the pressure build and relax in his sockets as the moist, confined space lubricated his eyes. Paulis blinked and suddenly found himself at the computer, which to his surprise, was placed next to his bed.

The dream woman was on his bed, restlessly sprawled out, naked, across a crisp white sheet. Her demeanor was more docile than usual, and there were no calculators covering her delicate places. The old high definition monitor highlighted the tawdry luster of her hair, which was lightly shaken to the sides. He moved the mouse around and noticed that the operating system was running slowly, and the antivirus software was turned off again.

The dream woman scraped her long, red nails across her upper torso and sensually stroked her body as she engaged him. “Paulis, I’m bleeding. Can you help me?”

Paulis was hypnotized by the rhythmic, heaving angles of her flesh and followed her hands as they trailed downward. She slowly allowed her legs to come apart, and he saw a trickle of blood stain the white sheets. “Come on, Paulis, you can do it. Help me.”

Did she want to have sex? Paulis was paralyzed with confusion.

The dream woman reached into her navel and withdrew an attached USB cable, pulling it in his direction with one smooth wave of her hand. Paulis intuitively took the cable and plugged it into the back of his computer. The shoebox tops on the walls quivered and contracted while the overhead lights dimmed. His computer hummed like a well oiled engine, as his desktop transformed into a live abdominal sonogram. Paulis stared at her briefly, but then retreated back to his computer.

The dream woman became more demanding and in control like she normally was, never taking her bold gaze away from him. Then she grabbed her abdomen and shook it. “Paulis, I’m bleeding. Help me.”

Her movements were reflected on his computer monitor. “Paulis, it’s not moving. Get it out!”

He watched, bewildered, as she tugged at her abdomen and a fetus violently shook from side to side on the computer screen.

“Get it out, it’s not moving!” she demanded.

He studied the gray image on the screen, its underdeveloped body crammed into a tight ball. At a loss and trying to figure out what she wanted, he selected the lifeless abdominal mass with the mouse, and dragged it to the trash can icon on his desktop. Then the dream woman howled, as thick ropes of blood skeeted from between her legs.

Startled, Paulis jumped from his seat and watched as a fully developed man’s head emerged from her parted legs. The massive head was attached to a partially formed, lifeless body that popped out with a sticky splash. Paulis wondered if this freak of nature was his child.

The shoebox tops on the walls expanded like hyperventilating lungs, while Paulis worked to maintain his own breathing at a normal pace. At first he thought he saw the baby move, but quickly realized it was just the gook separating away from its body. He stared in horror as the thick mucus slid away from the dead baby's head, to reveal his father's hairy face. A rancid smell of decay collapsed upon the room.

Panicked, Paulis heard someone knock at his bedroom door, and then the door knob shook. The dream woman was gone, but her remnants were everywhere. How would he explain this situation to whoever lurked beyond the door?

He grabbed the stilled baby and awkwardly tried to shove it into his backpack, periodically glancing in the direction of the door. A few salty beads of sweat trickled from his brow into his right eye, and down the bridge of his nose. His head raced, cluttered with unrealistic notions of how to explain himself. He lost his grip and the baby fell, head first, to the oak floor. The dull thud it made alarmed him. The skull was softer than it appeared. He expected to see it splatter everywhere, but to his surprise it was still intact. Again, he tried to shove it into his backpack, and after what seemed like an eternity, he finally realized that the bag was jammed with textbooks. He removed the books and carefully concealed the body in the backpack. He neatly folded the soiled sheets and slid them deep underneath the bed. While under the bed, he grabbed the computer power cord and snatched it from the wall, shutting the computer down.

Suddenly, the door rattled loudly on its hinges, and the hairs on the back of his neck rose in agony. He carefully strapped the heavy backpack over his shoulders, preparing for whatever was next. Then he struggled with the unnerving jolt he felt when a tiny hand cupped his spine through the thin fabric of the bag, and the baby moved against his back.

When he awoke, he peeled his head from the sweaty pillow, and decided it was time to take the risk and tell his parents what was happening. This time, they would listen, or he would make them regret it.

Chapter 19

Roree and Sarah sat in the therapist's waiting room, wondering what was being made of their son. Roree was motionless, with only his index finger flicking away at his tablet, even though intrusive thoughts about his work continued to shine through. Sarah's eyes relaxed into the warm colors of the room. The wool Berber carpet had deep, rich colors normally found only in synthetic fibers. With its ambient lighting and soothing music, Sarah felt more like she was in a living room, than a waiting room. She was glad they had decided to bring Paulis in for this unscheduled visit. They wanted everything for their son, and didn't want to take any chances with his development.

The students of Dimensions normally were required to see the translational psychiatrist every two weeks, once they started receiving the downloads. The psychological implications associated with research, designed to irreversibly alter cognitive function, had already been well documented in China. However, the credibility of China's reported findings was questionable, and thus an ongoing concern. At the school, the biweekly sessions were required, due to the experimental nature of the educational process. The purpose of the psychiatric visit was to counsel the child through any emotional changes, and to help them distinguish between that which was normal, relative to their peers, and that with which they should be concerned. It was also an opportunity to collect pertinent data.

Dr. Enzo De Luca was a translational clinical psychiatrist. This medical subspecialty had emerged with the acceptance of studies focused on human subjects, shifting toward post-humanism. Post-humanism was an ideology held by forward thinkers who sought to enhance human psychological and intellectual capacities. The individuals who populated these circles had made respectable strides, but it had proven to be a slow process. The creative team at Dimensions had figured out the next step. They had successfully created a carbon-based neurotransplant delivery system, with limitations bound only by the software engineer's imagination.

Dr. De Luca was a short, chubby, Italian man with an adorable air of sincerity. He casually strolled into the room with a tablet tucked under his arm. "Hello, Mr. Blunt. What brings you in this afternoon?"

Paulis was a little ashamed to have caused so much trouble and anxiously wondered if he would be able to tell the whole truth. "I think I failed my exams the other day."

Dr. De Luca took a seat and pulled up Paulis's test results. "Paulis, try not to worry too much about your exams. I can see from our dual scoring system that you agonized and second guessed yourself through the entire exam."

Paulis looked confused.

"It's normal to be a little nervous during an exam. You know, you had one hundred percent of the questions correct. Then you went back and changed your answers, which resulted in you only getting eighty percent. We always go with your first score, to see if the downloads were successful. The second score is your confidence score and this is where you need to focus. Just relax and trust your instincts. Keep practicing and let the information that's already there, come from you."

Paulis exhaled quietly. "So, what's the deal with this new vaccine I've been hearing about?"

Dr. De Luca was aware that the students knew about a vaccine. He was only allowed to explain the basics so he wouldn't get them too excited. "It allows you to transfer your downloaded information to your offspring."

"I know that. How does the vaccine work?"

Dr. De Luca dreaded these types of questions. "The vaccine works like a retrovirus, so it takes over the cells in the brain's pituitary gland. Then it creates a factory that produces follicle-stimulating hormone (FSH) which travels to your testes. There, it modifies the DNA and stimulates sperm maturation, but with the desired alterations, which allow your memories to carry over with your DNA."

Paulis smiled, pleased with the depth of his explanation. "How does that allow my sperm to get altered so that it carries my memories?"

"It injects its own ribonucleic acid (RNA), which translates into proteins that produce the mutated FSH. The hormone looks the same on the outside, so the testicle receptors recognize it as normal. Once the target is reached, the mutated FSH stimulates the production of the genetically corrected sperm."

"Why do the downloads work?"

"The information piggybacks along ascending neuron tracts from the finger to the brain. The vaccine will follow the same path, once it's programmed into a download. It will be downloaded the same way as any of your lessons."

"How does it find the proper target and become a memory?"

"That's proprietary information." Dr. De Luca smiled warmly.

Paulis frowned and thought to himself that even here in the doctor's office, he couldn't get a straight answer.

"Let's talk about your relationships. Your parents say you seem to be pulling away from others. Isolation can be dangerous at this stage in your development."

"Why is that?" asked Paulis.

"Do you feel like you're pulling away from others?"

"No, I just don't think they understand what I'm about."

"What are you about?"

"I just want a little inner peace. Is that too much to ask?"

"Inner peace?"

"Yes, peace!" said Paulis, as he breathed heavily.

"I hear you," said Dr. De Luca, in a calming tone. "Paulis, you've only befriended three people since you started at Dimensions."

"Who's counting?"

"You're doing the counting on your phone."

Paulis looked surprised.

"There are no secrets at Dimensions. Who you add or don't add to your network is recorded on your phone. You can learn a great deal about yourself through the interactions you have with others."

"I guess I also need to learn the difference between proprietary and secrets."

"I suspect you already know that. I'm trying to get you to participate in today's experience and learn more about yourself."

"Why do you care about my experience?"

"I believe it could give you a sense of being part of something. I think you already know you're part of something special."

Paulis studied him with ease.

"I know you've been asked these questions before, but let's review them again. Have you ever thought of harming yourself?"

"No."

"Do you take any medications or recreational drugs?"

"No."

"Do you plan to harm anyone in anyway?"

"No."

"Do you have possession of a gun or automatic weapon?"

"No."

"Do you own or are you building a bomb?"

"No."

"Are you collecting any harmful chemicals?"

Paulis laughed. "No."

The physician smiled and leaned in. "Are you sure?"

"Yes, I'm sure."

He noted that Paulis's affect was normal and he was properly engaged. "Do you hear voices?"

Paulis paused. "Not when I'm awake. Well, I hear people when they're speaking to me but not voices in my head." Then he crossed his arms and searched Dr. De Luca's face.

"What happens here stays between you and me." said Dr. De Luca.

Paulis closed his eyes and exhaled deeply. "There's this woman in my dreams. She knows what I do when I'm awake, and punishes me for it."

"Punishes you, how?"

Paulis blushed. “She withholds affection if I’m with another girl.”

“Another girl, like Terry?”

Paulis was surprised by his question. “Yes. I guess she gets jealous.”

“Jealous, how?”

He quietly fidgeted in his seat.

“Do you have wet dreams?” asked Dr. De Luca.

Paulis smiled shyly. “Yes, I guess you could say that.”

“How would you say it?”

“What you said is fine.”

Dr. De Luca gave him a reassuring nod. “I have a special download for you. It will help you control what happens in your dreams, or at least you’ll know that it’s only a dream when it’s happening. Just login tonight after 8:00 p.m., and your prescription should be ready for downloading. Of course, let me know if your problem is not resolved.”

“So, I’m not crazy?”

“You’re a tremendous young man. You just need a good night’s sleep. Sometimes the downloads can interfere with that." Dr. De Luca stood up and patted Paulis on the shoulder. "Keep up the good work, and good luck with Terry. I'm sure she will forgive you." He then gave Paulis the tablet, and left him alone to complete the office visit questionnaire.

After hearing the doctor's comments, he thought about how he had hurt Terry's feelings the other day. He felt like he was becoming a horrible person. He knew he had to make it up to her, but he just didn't know how.

He completed the form, making a conscious effort not to change his answers, and then went to look for his parents. When Paulis entered the waiting room, his parents both immediately rose and studied his posture. Paulis smiled, sensing their concern, and walked over to welcome their warm embrace.

"Let's go for lobsters!" said Roree.

Sarah was relieved to see Paulis smile. He hadn't seemed happy for many days. Her family was everything to her, and she was delighted that they were all together to celebrate Paulis's good news.

Sarah's parents used to take her out after getting a checkup or immunization, to celebrate good health and family cohesiveness. Then her father went away, and the happy family moments stopped. She recalled how her mother had changed after her father left. It appeared that overnight, Vivian had become this overprotective, self-righteous security guard, sporting steel-toed pumps. She was always there for her, but no single woman could be everything.

One thing was certain; she sure couldn't accuse Vivian of not trying. Sarah had always heard that being adopted was a gift and a blessing, but somehow it didn't seem that way. She needed to hear how it all came to be in order for her to understand who she was. She needed it to come from Vivian for it to be real.

---The Study---

Vivian was online in the Blunt family study, researching the current statutes regarding liability in coma cases. She was trying to decide if she wanted to offer her assistance to Shelly's family. More importantly, she was worried that she might find herself with a conflict of interest, if she dug deep enough to reach what she suspected to be the truth.

While working on the computer, she noticed a PDF document titled, "Genetic Analysis Report- S. Blunt." Without hesitation, she opened the document and quickly learned that Sarah now had the DNA results, which showed that they were not related. She began to panic before remembering that the DNA analysis was only part of the story. She read the rest of the lab report and saw that Dr. Babette Jones was listed as the ordering physician. There was a second PDF document titled, "Restraining Order: Babette Jones vs. Vivian Cooper Final Order of Protection." She clutched her stomach as a wave of nausea engulfed her body.

"What was Roree doing with this, and what was Babette doing back in their lives?" she thought to herself. "Babette, Babette Jones." She held her breath, hoping to deactivate the swelling urgency poised to erupt. Then she threw her hand to her mouth and ran to the bathroom, giving back her expensive lunch.

She rinsed out her mouth and shook her head, unable to dislodge the image from her brain. She remembered that Babette was a few years younger, her hair was longer, and she came from money. Babette's delicate frame, which lived in conflict with her voluptuous demeanor, taunted Vivian today just as clearly as it had done in the past. The jealousy had reared its uncombed head, and like with any horrible train wreck, she couldn't look away. She lunged forward and dry heaved over the sink.

When Vivian first met Babette, she didn't care for her arrogance, but respected her professionally. It wasn't until they shook hands, that something told her Babette's soul was not bound by the fear of God.

Vivian had flown from Detroit to Boston to surprise her husband on one of his many business trips. On some level, she knew his company was too cheap to pay for the Ritz-Carlton, where he claimed to be staying. Only the elite, refined Negroes got to stay at the Ritz, so she needed to see this place for herself. When she arrived at the hotel she learned that Wayne, her husband, was not staying at the hotel alone. The front desk explained that he and his wife had taken in a matinee and she had just missed them. Vivian contained herself, unwilling to jump to any untoward conclusion. However, she was not without a plan.

She walked around the outside of the hotel and found the service entrance. She talked her way in, and then generously bribed one of the maids to let her into their room. She knew she was going to need hard-core evidence, if she was going to accuse her husband of adultery. When she walked into the suite, she was immediately taken aback by the room's posh elegance and the expensive artwork. The crown molding and attention to detail were only sullied by the lipstick-stained champagne glasses and the negligee that had been cast carelessly to the floor.

She walked out of that room on the dark side of reason, and stumbled out into the cold streets of Boston. Vivian was determined not to be that classless bitch that caused a nasty scene at the Ritz. She inconspicuously perched across the street in the Public Gardens until they finally returned.

Based on past interactions, Babette was not the woman she expected to see hanging off her man's arm. Yet there she was, just as bold as day. Vivian momentarily shivered into a steamy cup of coffee, weakened with anger and confusion. Then she got pissed!

She flew home and packed and unpacked Wayne's belongings several times, before finally deciding to wait until he returned. He was the father of her seven-year-old daughter, and Vivian loved him in the most vulnerable way. She would confront him, and propose that they get marriage counseling to handle this situation like civilized Christians; after all, she was a lawyer and a shrewd negotiator. Unfortunately, when he returned, the negotiations deteriorated into begging, and finally a restraining order. The Devil was a clever deceiver and he had come to steal, kill and destroy. Forty years later, nothing had changed. Vivian couldn't understand why this woman was back in their lives.

Chapter 20

Sarah was in her pajamas, video chatting with friends she recently made on an MS chat site. Unlocking the vast resources of the MS community had provided the support and knowledge she needed to make her new reality tolerable. Her aimless anxiety had been replaced with a sense of empowerment, once she understood what to expect from her illness. She was also excited that her father was coming to visit, and had been reminiscing about her childhood, when they were a happy family.

Wayne had contacted her out of concern, after getting a request for information regarding his family history. The doctors indicated that they needed to include his detailed history, for Sarah's genetic analysis to be complete.

Vivian wasn't as excited as Sarah was about the prospect of Wayne seeping back into their lives. Paulis had told her how his relationship had developed with her ex-husband on Facebook, despite her unrelenting warnings that the man was an unfit human being. Paulis thought he was playing matchmaker when he gave her Wayne's phone number. He failed to imagine anything that Wayne could have done to sustain such a lifetime of hatred.

Over the last few months, he had learned that his grandfather had other children and grandchildren. This meant he had cousins, and an extended family he knew nothing about, but was now meeting through Facebook. He had endless fantasies related to who his grandfather was and how it framed who he would become. Paulis feared his grandfather's return might cause problems he couldn't foresee or reverse. Of course, his burning curiosity exceeded his fear of that which may not be. On the other hand, maybe there was a reason Vivian took such extremes to exclude Wayne from their lives.

Vivian peeked into Sarah's room. "Is everything ok in here?"

"Yes, mother, I'm fine," said Sarah, but she never took her eyes away from the screen.

"Ok, good night." Vivian was glad to hear that Sarah was still calling her "mother," though she thought it was rude, how the younger generations were constantly connected to their latest vice. Vivian took a sip from her wine glass as she made her way down the hall to the guest room.

Paulis's meddling had angered Vivian, after all she had done for her family as a single parent. Of course, she understood that Paulis didn't have enough information to deduce the fact that her ex-husband was a slithering snake. Nevertheless, Vivian was not about to allow Wayne to unravel the delicate tapestry she had struggled so hard to maintain.

Vivian reluctantly picked up the phone to call Wayne. She felt an unexpected tug at her heart as she dialed the number. It was so suffocating that she had to disconnect the call. It had been over thirty years since she threw him out; since he last stroked her body with his domineering caress. She had to fight to forget the love they shared, so she could stay strong and get through the call.

Wayne had treated her like she had the word Mattel tattooed across her ass, but Vivian was nobody's toy. She didn't regret throwing him out, because otherwise, she would have tortured him at every opportunity. It was clear that she couldn't forgive him, so she had to let him go.

Once again, she punched his number into the phone. Now that her memory was refreshed with the full picture, she could stand tall, without getting caught up.

A baritone voice answered. "Hello, Vivian. How have you been? I thought I might be hearing from you."

"I'm fine. How did you know it was me?"

"Paulis gave me your number, so I put it in my phone. You should hear the ring tone I chose for your number." He laughed, and then there was an awkward moment of silence. "So, how's our Sarah doing?"

"She's fine, considering."

"You know, I'm coming to see her. I think it's time."

"Wayne, I don't think that's such a good idea."

"Vivian, before you make a hasty decision…"

Vivian interrupted with a deep breath. "Let me be clear. You better answer that genetic questionnaire right there, from the confines of wherever the fuck you've been for the last thirty years!"

"Vivian, you're not scaring anybody with that tone. I don't need your permission. Isn't there an ounce of forgiveness or compassion in your heart, after all these years?"

"No! You used that up when you stepped out on me; when you stepped out on us. Did you know that woman is in contact with Sarah? Don't you dare come around here after all this time!"

"No, I wasn't aware of that. The doctors said they need a blood sample..."

"And that's exactly what they're gonna get, if you show your face around here!" She disconnected the call, piping hot with fury.

Roree was standing at the doorway and had overheard Vivian's argument with Wayne. He caught her by the elbow as she came marching out of the room. "When are you gonna tell Sarah the truth?"

"You don't know what you're talking about," said Vivian. She stared him up and down, before focusing on the sweaty hand that clutched her arm.

Her face was puffy, and he could have sworn one of the tiny spider veins on her cheek menacingly threatened to pop in his direction. "Is there a reason you think you should keep her father away? She could use his support through all of the stuff she's going through," said Roree.

"That's *your* job. Now, get off me!" shouted Vivian, as she jerked her arm away.

"Sarah's not gonna be pleased to hear about this. You know, Paulis has been chatting with him on Facebook for months now."

"Yes, he told me. You need to have more control over who that boy is communicating with online."

"There's no harm in him getting to know his grandfather." Roree smiled as he spoke.

Hearing the term "grandfather" wrecked her nerves; Wayne had not earned that title. "You're being irresponsible. He's only fifteen!"

"You know, Paulis is smarter than you give him credit," said Roree.

"I give him plenty of credit. Your competency as a parent is what's questionable."

"Well, that's really none of your business. All you need to know is that we've got it covered."

"I'm sure the parents of that girl, who ended up in a coma, thought they had it covered, too." She paused, allowing her words a moment to penetrate. "I was reading that her grandfather had a controversial investment deal with someone named Blunt. Was that your father?"

"I don't know anything about that," said Roree.

She scrutinized him carefully. "Yes, I'm sure you don't. Paulis also told me he took that girl's place. It was very lucky for him that a space became available in the second year class."

Roree boldly met her gaze, as his stomach soured and quietly deceived him. "Yes, it was. I guess life is really a zero-sum game; somebody falls, and then somebody else rises to take their place."

"Aren't you the least bit curious about how she fell? After all, your son is being exposed to the same thing."

"Actually, I'm not. All we really know is that she was doing something she wasn't supposed to be doing."

Vivian aggressively swept her hair behind her ear. "Did she wake up and tell you that herself? I just don't buy it, as tightly as that place is wrapped. It doesn't explain anything and quite frankly it's inexplicable!" She moved past him in the hallway. "I wouldn't be the least bit surprised, if the answer lies on somebody's computer, or a database where that rogue download got authorized. There's always an electronic footprint, so you'd better govern yourself accordingly."

"Don't you think the school and those sniping lawyers already covered that?" He smirked, mocking her enthusiasm.

"I'm sure they did, but they did a poor job." She eyeballed him dismissively. "That's why I've offered to represent the family pro-bono." She turned and stormed away.

Roree nervously laughed out loud. "Well, good luck with that." He was shocked by how excited she was at the prospect of digging into this issue. She was the most vivacious he had seen her in years; it was disgusting. Too bad it was all rooted in her hatred for him. It had nothing to do with concern for the family she was going to represent. His pulse throbbed as he thought about how he'd like to peel back her scalp and vacuum the racist debris from her gaping skull. However, that was not the man he wanted to be and that was not who he would become. He walked in the opposite direction to his bedroom, where Sarah was preparing for bed.

"Your mother, if that's what we're still calling her, is representing the family of that girl in the coma."

"Shelly's family. Good, it will keep her out of my hair. I've got bigger things on my mind, at the moment. I'm still trying to get the vaccine ready on time," said Sarah, as she turned down the sheets and climbed into bed.

"She suspects that I had something to do with it."

She paused, noting the urgency in his voice. "What exactly did she say?"

"She mumbled something about my computer being evidence, and my soul burning from internal damnation. You know how she thinks."

"You mean your soul burning in eternal damnation." She smiled, but Roree was not amused. "It sounds like she's fishing. If she had a shred of evidence, she'd be doing a victory lap, and you would already be behind bars." Sarah laughed. "She only barks if she can't get away with the bite."

Roree looked out the window when he heard Vivian's car door slam. "Why does she hate me so much?"

"Maybe if you didn't take the bait and try to antagonize her..."

Roree looked at her in total disbelief. "She just told your father to never show his face around here. You know what that woman's like after she's had a bottle of wine. She only told me about the lawsuit because she thinks I've discovered something related to your adoption."

"Is that what she said?" This angered Sarah. She was finally going to be reunited with her father and she didn't intend to let anything or anybody stand in the way, including Vivian!

Roree clutched his fist. "No, not exactly."

Sarah felt her head begin to stir. It had been a while since she thought about how Roree put Shelly in a coma, and then rationalized that poor girl's good health to mere collateral damage. Though it benefited their son, she didn't approve of his tactics. She couldn't deny that Paulis wouldn't be in this school if her husband wasn't willing to take risks, so she let it go. Now, the truth had come to claim its place, as it always did.

Maybe if she spoke to her mother, she could straighten the whole thing out; the adoption, and Vivian's bad blood with Roree. Though she was adopted and the truth had been kept from her all these years, Wayne was the only father she ever knew. Vivian owed her something. Maybe she would be open to reason. Sarah knew that once one's ego and the superficial barriers were stripped away, everybody had a price. She would have to appeal to what Vivian held as important. The problem was, Vivian always held her cards close, and would never allow herself to be exposed enough to reveal what that price was.

"There's something your mother doesn't want you to know, and I think it goes deeper than you being adopted," said Roree.

"Oh, please, not everybody is as twisted as you," said Sarah.

"Maybe not, but I think this is more than Vivian being a self-righteous bitch in the name of Jesus. She's afraid of something. You'd better talk to her before I lose my patience and things get out of hand."

"We will see about that," said Sarah, as she studied his face, translating the subtext intertwined with his words. "You stay here."

She grabbed the phone and punched in her mother's number. After several rings she answered. "Mother, I hope you're not planning on going home. You've had too much wine to be driving." Sarah walked down the stairs as she spoke on the phone.

Moments later, Vivian re-entered the house and dropped her keys in the big bowl on the table by the door. "I can hold my alcohol like a proper lady. I don't know what you're worried about."

"What is going on with you and Roree?"

"Oh, and here I thought you were concerned about me."

Sarah locked the door. “Mother, what are you two fighting about?”

Vivian pointed her shaking finger upstairs. “I’ve always felt like that man’s spirit was troubled. I thought it was because of his upbringing, but now I know better. He’s lost his way and I don’t believe that you, his work, or even the Lord can bring him back.”

Sarah stared at her, hopelessly. “I thought you believed that God could see the good in all of us?”

“My faith in the Lord is strong, but you’ve got to open your heart to receive his wonderful blessings. Roree’s smug stance needs to shake until his shackles of logic serve him no more! Only then will the angels rejoice, and the vultures lose sight of their prey.”

Sarah rolled her eyes indignantly. She was not in the mood for one of her mother’s liquor sermons. “I love my husband, and you need to respect that! My family means everything to me.”

“I’m not your family?”

Sarah just stared, confused about how to respond.

“Oh, I see,” said Vivian, as she pushed past her to grab her car keys.

Sarah stood in front of the table. “Mother, you’ve had too much.”

"Don't give me that self-righteous crap! You think I don't know about the shit that's going on at that school? If you weren't my daughter, you might be behind bars. Why don't you think about that while you stand in judgment of me."

Vivian removed her coat and moved to go up to the guest room.

"You know, unfounded accusations like that could bring us all under unnecessary scrutiny."

Vivian quietly ascended the stairs without looking back.

Sarah watched, wondering if her mother was just drunk or seriously threatening her. She finally went back upstairs and climbed into bed. She turned to Roree, and shook her head in resignation before turning off the lamp. "She just needs to sleep it off."

"Yes, I'm sure that will solve all of her problems." He lightly ran his fingers across her shoulders, and gazed into her eyes as his vision slowly adjusted to the dark.

"Roree, you can't be serious."

Roree aggressively ran his fingers through her hair and pulled her resistant body close, taking in the heated scent of her sweat. He gently collapsed his mouth over her full lips, rubbing his nose against hers. After a few seconds, he parted his lips and slid his tongue into her mouth. Sarah sighed, and passionately darted her tongue against his, feeling his rough whiskers slowly rotate and tingle her face. Then she moaned, and cupped his shoulders as she relaxed into his embrace.

He ran his hands down her torso, resting them on her firm buttocks. "Are you getting any closer to completing the vaccine?" asked Roree.

"I'm on track to deliver it on time," said Sarah, slightly breathless. "You think you're gonna be able to upload it without putting anybody else in a coma?" asked Sarah sarcastically, before lightly biting into his lower lip.

He flinched and pulled his face back, tasting a brief hint of salt as a few drops of blood interspersed with their saliva. "What's that supposed to mean?" asked Roree.

Sarah stared him in the face blankly, for a moment.

"You just handle your part, and I'll handle mine," said Roree. He rolled her onto her back and thrust his wanting hard-on into her pelvis. Sarah groaned and bucked gently under his weight, putting aside all of her problems and uncertainties. She released her inhibitions as her body reawakened, and her desire carried her to that place she thought had been lost forever.

Chapter 21

Sarah had arranged a girl's afternoon at the day spa, for herself and Vivian. She chose the Harmony suite because it had walls of water that cascaded quietly in the background. Soothing music and the aromas of lavender and peppermint swirled throughout the room. They had just received deep tissue massages and were relaxed, drinking chilled Chi coconut tea.

Sarah stared at her mother, whose eyelids were covered with cucumbers. She wondered how she could be so relaxed and peaceful, with all of her vile secrets. Then the words erupted out of her, like a tea kettle whistling to completion. "Mother, there's something you've been keeping from me, and I want to know what it is, right now."

"Watch the tone, and what are you accusing me of this time?" Vivian was using her ghetto voice.

"I'm adopted." She had lowered her voice, hoping Vivian would do the same. She waited for her to show some emotion, but Vivian didn't budge.

"I'm still your mother." Vivian paused, innocently. "Why do you insist on draining the joy from everything?"

Sarah whispered through clenched teeth. "I could see you keeping it from me until I was old enough to understand, but for God's sake, I'm in my forties; you had no right!" She aggressively scanned her mother's façade, as if searching for a logical explanation.

Vivian raised her hands to the Lord. "Some things should just be left alone. You're my daughter, my gift. What difference does anything else make?"

"I know you're my mother, but I have a right to know who I am! Wouldn't you want to know? If I had known the truth, maybe we could have gained some insight into my neurological condition, before I nearly killed myself, driving the car into a guardrail! If it wasn't for Dr. Jones, I would still be in the dark."

Vivian propped herself up on her elbows, and the cucumbers fell from her eyes. She hopelessly searched for the empathy to process Sarah's remarks and then her posture changed. "So, your geneticist is Dr. Jones?"

"Yes," said Sarah.

"Babette Jones?"

"Yes, Babette Jones!" Sarah was becoming annoyed with her mother's attempt to derail the topic, and escape responsibility for her actions.

Vivian exhaled heavily. "Let me tell you about your mother." She sat up, smudging her mud mask. "I couldn't conceive because my fallopian tubes were scarred. So, your father and I decided to consult a fertility specialist here in Boston, and began traveling from Detroit for treatments. Eventually, we decided to do artificial insemination."

"Oh, I didn't know that," said Sarah.

Vivian looked at her straight on, and exhaled indignantly. "There's a lot you don't know. They were supposed to combine my eggs and your father's sperm, and implant the embryos in me."

Sarah seemed a little relieved, but then her face hardened. "I know how it works, but that doesn't explain why our blood types don't match!"

Vivian froze for a moment, and then her body shook, as a tear dropped violently from her face. She didn't seem to know she was crying. "Well, instead of using my eggs, she used her own."

"Oh dear God, was it a mix-up?" asked Sarah, horrified.

Vivian's posture morphed into a smoldering rage. Now, the tears streamed defenselessly down her cheeks, and her voice quivered. "This was no mix-up! At the time, I didn't know that the woman I trusted to handle the procedure was your father's vindictive, little piece."

"Babette?" whispered Sarah.

Vivian avoided her stare. "She used me like a disposable Petri dish!"

"That sick bitch!" exclaimed Sarah. She had never witnessed her mother in such a diminished state. "Why didn't you have her arrested?"

"I threatened to kill them both, but she took out a restraining order against me. I should have killed her when I had the chance." She lowered her voice and held her head in her hands, taking a moment to collect herself. "It was the seventies, and I had already tampered with God's will. I was just too embarrassed for this to come out. This was not something the church would have been able to overlook. Back then, divorce was already a big enough scandal. I just wanted them out of our lives. I never did maternity, testing because I knew you were my daughter, and no blood test was going to change that."

"But it changes everything!" said Sarah, hysterically. "Did Daddy know this was happening?" Sarah had lost her breath in utter shock. Her wide eyes were still focused on her poor mother.

"You need to calm down!"

Sarah settled back and took several deep breaths, but still looked to her for answers.

"He confessed that their affair started before I became pregnant, but he didn't know she was doing anything abusive toward me. I discovered their affair only after you were seven years old. He said he would break it off, if I could find it in my heart to forgive him. When he tried to leave her, she threatened to tell me that you weren't mine. Instead of being blackmailed, he decided to tell me the whole story."

Vivian hung her head in defeat. "Your father didn't know, but he was weak, and he allowed that tart to blind him with her flesh." Vivian wiped her face with a crumpled tissue. "You were a blessing, and you're all I've got. That woman has no place in our lives or in anybody else's."

Sarah sat quietly, catching her breath. The more she thought about the pivotal interactions she'd had with Babette, since her hospitalization, the more irrational her thought processes became. Calling her birth a blessing or a gift from God was Vivian's spin. It was designed to categorize something, for which there was no name. When God brought two people together, they created a child to reflect the beauty of his master plan. This is how she viewed the beautiful son she created with Roree. Sarah's existence was created out of something dirty and spiteful. How could anything good have come from that? But what if she was the proverbial diamond in the rough? What if her work was actually God's work, and she was a mere conduit? Perhaps her coldly calculated life journey was not without purpose.

"So she's been manipulating me all this time? You know, she's Terry's grandmother, and she's involved with Paulis's school! Why would she do such a horrible thing?"

Vivian leaned in close, "because that bitch is crazy. You'd better be careful not to allow your emotions to cloud your judgment."

Sarah knew she had to get past this. Her mother's behavior towards Roree, and anything remotely related to science, was beginning to make sense. However, her decision to play victim all her life was no excuse to make everybody else miserable. She never imagined the day would come that she saw Vivian as a victim. She now realized that the harder she pounded, the more the layers would peel away from Vivian's tough façade. At the core, there could be a woman with whom she could possibly reason. Somehow, this information gave Sarah a sense of control.

"So, he's my real father?" asked Sarah.

"That man was no father to you, and I told you, we never did genetic testing." Vivian's heart sank. "How did you get the DNA to test me in the first place?"

"I thought you gave it to the hospital when I was admitted. Is that why you've been keeping my father and me apart? You think you're gonna lose your place, if his bloodline is thicker than yours?"

"Don't be ridiculous! You think there's a blood test that's gonna neatly summarize the shit I just dropped on you? All my life, I've tried to give my best, and what did I get in return?"

An attendant in white smocks came in with warm blankets and fresh tea. She quickly left them in peace, having sensed she interrupted something. Sarah digested Vivian's comments as she poured them both fresh cups of tea, and offered her a warm blanket.

"I can understand why you kept that from me, but I decide who I have in my life, and who I call family."

Vivian had regained her customary, judgmental composure as she clutched the warm blanket to her neck. "I'm not your family?"

"I'll answer that after I've had time to process all of your lies."

Vivian replaced the cucumbers over her eyes, and sighed with resolve as she reclined back into place. Then she opened her fist to the ceiling, as if she were releasing delicate butterflies upon their maiden journey. "You know what they say, the truth shall set you free."

"Excuse me, I think I need some fresh air," said Sarah as she got up and went to the locker room.

Chapter 22

Johanna and Babette had parked the car earlier that afternoon, so they could wander the narrow streets of one of Boston's most historic neighborhoods, before meeting Sarah at Guscio. The North End was fabulous, and Babette loved the energy she got whenever she went there. Mike's Pastries was a naughty bonus that nobody could resist, and though the line was often stretched up the block, it was well worth the wait. Johanna had to practically drag her from the pastry shop line, or they never would have made it to dinner.

Johanna had found the pep in her step today, and was excited to be there with Babette and Sarah. She hadn't taken a Percocet in over five hours, so she was lucid. She was ready to discuss the children's future and embrace the changes they were about to unleash upon the world.

In the beginning, Johanna was uncomfortable with Terry having the gay gene. Now, gay or straight, she would still have grandchildren; that's what she really longed for. Furthermore, due to the vaccine Sarah was creating, her grandchildren would be born pre-loaded with brilliance! She was glad that Babette had talked her into allowing her daughter to become a part of Dimensions.

Sarah was a little uneasy about meeting with Johanna and Babette, now that she knew Babette was her biological mother. She was supposed to be angry, but she wasn't sure it was the appropriate emotion. Anger required conscious energy, especially if your heart wasn't in it. She knew that being in Babette's presence would inevitably elicit a visceral response. When all else failed, her gut would tell her the truth.

Now that she had taken the time to think about it, she was certainly impressed with Vivian. Of course, she had her jagged edges, but she kept her composure. Somehow, she maintained order for all those years and move past her horrible situation. Most women would have lost it, but Vivian kept her faith, and pressed forward. Trials and tribulations were more than a catchphrase for her. When Vivian testified, it was from a place of tested faith.

Johanna and Babette entered the restaurant and moved straight to the front of the line. Babette shimmied out of her gray Cape Blazer, capturing the immediate attention of the women working the podium. The maitre d' showed the ladies to their seats on the second floor of the restaurant, where Sarah had been waiting. The hip world music and dark ambience of Guscio made you feel as if you were part of a play, instead of merely meeting for dinner. Sarah watched Babette as she took her seat.

They exchanged pleasantries, and bragged about Terry's and Paulis's progress in school. The children had made up and were back together again. Meanwhile, Sarah tried to imagine what approach Babette had taken to seduce her father, so many years ago. She couldn't believe she had the gall to do what Vivian accused her of doing.

"Can I start you ladies with some drinks?" asked the waiter. Babette watch him carefully, noting his clean-cut demeanor and pitch-black, shiny, Italian hair.

Sarah leaned back. "I'll have a cosmopolitan."

Babette suggestively ran a finger along the smooth, leather edges of her menu. "Shirley Temple, please."

"I'll have a dirty martini," said Johanna, as she opened her napkin and plopped it into her lap.

The waiter recited the evening's specials, salivating with each description as if he had just sampled each one. Then he left with their drink orders.

"So, Sarah, how's the vaccine coming along?" asked Johanna.

Sarah noticed that Johanna was more engaged and present than usual. "I had to make a few changes to what we proposed, but it's progressing rather well." She smiled.

"Last time we met, you said the downloaded information that the children obtained in their short-term memory would be passed down to their offspring, right?" asked Johanna.

"Actually, it's the information that's saved to their long-term memory that will be transferred to their offspring," said Sarah.

"If that's still true, then what are the changes you've made?" asked Babette.

"Well, the vaccine still works like a retrovirus. However, once it's converted all of the host DNA, they will become sterile. The students will be sterile to everyone, except those or decedents of those inoculated with the same vaccine. At least, that's what happened to the rats."

"You mean sterile to the rest of the world!" said Johanna, in a panic.

"The vaccine will alter the DNA as we planned, but they will only be able to procreate with others who've had the same vaccine exposure. Yes, they become a new species only able to breed within their own. It has to start somewhere. Of course, this can't get out until we have the first set of seniors as living proof that it works, because the press is going to be fierce!" said Sarah, with a charged smile.

Babette's mouth fell open. "Sarah, I believe the board agreed to something a little different. What if something goes wrong, and they can't even breed with each other?"

"That's the price that comes with progress." Sarah stared at Babette's heaving bosom. "Well, I guess you better give it some thought, if you're going to get cold feet. Once we've created a new species, we can't reverse it. We can't just take it back."

Two bar-backs descended upon their table, and delivered their colorful drinks. The ladies were caught in an awkward silence, half-reading their menus, but at the same time mulling over Sarah's proposal. Sarah even had to retrace her words, which seemed to carry more weight, now that she had spoken them out loud.

Johanna had turned edgy. She felt like they were both talking down to her, like she was a child or an idiot. She knew she could handle this situation, but her concern was for her child. If something went wrong, she would never, ever forgive herself, and somebody would pay. She reached for her purse, but then changed her mind and put it back. Then she grabbed it again, fidgeting, as if she were about to unlatch a dormant volcano. It's not like she was a heroin addict, she thought to herself. It's prescription medication that she used, so it was totally safe. In the streets you never knew what you were getting, but with prescription medications, you had the FDA's seal of approval.

Johanna nonchalantly took two pills from her little, pearl pill box. She rubbed her nose and popped one in her mouth, and then she slipped the other one into her dirty martini. She briefly studied the ladies' faces, certain that no one had witnessed her swift maneuver. She followed the bubbles as the pill slowly drifted to the bottom of the glass. Then, she punched it repeatedly with a toothpick-speared olive.

"Hello, ladies, how are we doing with drinks?" asked the waiter.

Babette looked at Johanna's glass with a dead stare. "Our drinks are fine. I believe we're ready to order."

Babette ordered the asparagus and mushroom risotto, and Sarah ordered the salmon. Babette flirted with the waiter, as she would with any handsome man at her service, but he was focused on Johanna.

"Excuse me, ma'am, may I take your dinner order?"

"Of course, I'll have the filet mignon, medium rare," said Johanna, abruptly drawn out of her daydream. Johanna noticed Babette and the waiter exchange lingering glances as he read back their orders, and finally turned to leave the table.

"What about the pièce de résistance?" whispered Babette, in her worst French accent, as she obsessively watched him walk away.

They momentarily laughed to themselves, but Johanna couldn't help but notice how Sarah continued to stare in Babette's direction. The energy between the two of them had changed during her brief daydream. Johanna had begun to feel euphoric, but at the same time, she felt an undeniable wave of panic. She wasn't sure if her heart was racing from the drugs she mixed in with her martini, or if she had really heard Sarah just propose that her daughter become the first generation of a new species?

She had finally come to terms with the philosophies of Dimensions, and the higher intellectual being Terry was developing into. The ability her daughter would have to pass on her neurological and cognitive changes to the next generation fascinated her. It was the new element, of selective sterility, that was over-the-top and troubling. What had she allowed Babette to talk her into? All of these years, she had been living behind a prescription drug fog. To finally awaken, and find that her daughter was being exposed to something that could ruin her life, was making her feel helpless. She thought the possibility of Terry being gay or having cancer were big problems, but now, she realized these were just the natural draws of life. However, becoming a new species was uncharted territory, and it was scaring the living daylights out her.

"I'm not willing to take that kind of risk with my daughter," said Johanna. She rubbed her chest, in an attempt to contain her panic, which had threatened to erupt and run away with her. She took a sip from her martini, and suddenly felt a gentle detachment from her emotions.

Sarah was stunned to see how she chose to cope with her insecurities about this matter. She followed the cloudy martini as Johanna gently nursed it, like an elusive lover.

"Well it's not your decision, and it's not that simple!" said Babette. "You may feel differently in two years, when it's Terry's turn to be exposed." Babette gazed into Sarah's eyes with admiration. "Let's see how the seniors do this year, before we draw any hasty conclusions."

"Yes, Johanna, only your mother is allowed to decide the fate of mankind," said Sarah.

Johanna rubbed her nose and looked at Sarah with confusion. Babette stared into space for a moment, and then turned her focus on Sarah. "Is there something you'd like to say?" asked Babette.

Sarah leaned in towards Babette, and her voice began to quiver. "My mother told me about the little game you played with her and my father."

"What are you two talking about?" asked Johanna. She stared between Babette and Sarah, admiring the kaleidoscope images that the lights cast above their heads, like halos.

Babette's heart raced with panic. She wasn't ready for this moment, though she had been rehearsing for it since the day Sarah was born. "If you think I was just playing a little game, then what does that make you? I used cutting edge technology when I created you. You'll be telling your grandchildren the same thing some day; that is, if you can really pull off what you claim to be able to do."

Looking at Babette was like looking at an aged self-portrait. She hoped the day would never come, when her son felt the same disrespect that she felt for Babette. Sarah realized that no matter how legitimate her judgment felt, she was a product of Babette's disease. The generations to follow would also tell a story, except now, it would be her vaccine, and her disease that would be referenced. "What did you do with my mother's eggs?" asked Sarah.

"Of all the things you could ask! What did you think; I fed them to your father on a cracker with champagne, because he had a taste for the finer things in life?" She laughed playfully but Sarah didn't budge. "Theoretically, a patient's sample can be frozen and kept safe for years, but you already knew that."

"Is that how you got my mother's DNA to run that test? Because, she certainly didn't give it to you!"

"The DNA results are authentic. If Vivian wants to contest the lab work, then she can give a fresh sample of her DNA. You'll learn soon enough, that I don't get cold feet." She took a moment to draw in the undivided attention she had from her daughters. "Sarah, where would the world be without you? Like you said, it had to start somewhere." She searched for some reasoning in Sarah's rigid posture. "You know that invincible run of adrenalin you get when you think about changing the world? Well, I know that feeling too. I just don't want us to let things get out of hand."

Sarah received an unexpected jolt of excitement from Babette's words, but then her skin crawled, and her left thigh contracted painfully. She casually rubbed her leg. "That's some set of brass balls you've got there. You've been waiting for just the right moment to reveal this whole, sick thing, haven't you? Why now? How many people have you done this to?"

Babette became flushed with desperation, as she watched Sarah gloat in her discomfort. She also felt relieved that the truth was out. She knew she was eventually going to have to tell her, anyway. She was amazed at how much Sarah resembled her, in her youth. She felt for her, trying to imagine what this experience must be like; learning that Vivian was not really her mother, and accepting *her* as her new mother.

She thought about how her own mother committed suicide when she was only fourteen, and how she subsequently learned that her mother was never in her corner. Instead, she turned out to be a narcissist, who did everything she could to win her husband's love, even if it meant destroying her own daughter. Babette had earned her brass balls.

The work Sarah had done for Dimensions was impressive, and she was proud of her. Her daughter was becoming a pioneer of science. Then she felt the bite of Sarah's bitterness and hostility, tempered only by the fact that she understood it. "Sarah, I know you must hate me right now, but you will get over that. Look at you; you're brilliant!"

"What are you two talking on about? When I found out that I was adopted, I was relieved. My mother died during childbirth and Babette took me in as her own. Were you adopted, too?" asked Johanna.

"No, I wish it were that simple." She exhaled, and pointed her stiff finger at Babette. "Your mother, here, substituted her own eggs during artificial insemination procedures. Perhaps you should get a blood test, to see if she did the same thing to your parents," said Sarah.

"No need to do a blood test; Johanna knows all she has to do, is ask," said Babette.

Sarah looked at Johanna. "If I were you, I would get the blood test."

"Is this true?" asked Johanna. "Did my mother really die during childbirth?"

Babette studied Johanna's face, wondering what she was really asking. Then she chose her words carefully. "Yes, she did."

Johanna was drunk with confusion. Sarah and Babette were locked in quiet combat around the subject of Sarah's parents. The realization that Babette was Sarah's biological mother made Johanna feel jealous, because she was no longer the only woman in Babette's life.

Johanna had always been a low achiever, but managed to marry a successful man because of her good looks. Nevertheless, she was still lonely, because her husband was in pharmaceutical sales, and traveled abroad seventy-five percent of the year. Though she would never admit it, she suspected he preferred it that way. She also felt like an inadequate parent, but luckily, her daughter turned out fine. However, she couldn't take responsibility for any of Terry's successes. The respect she received from Babette was dogmatic, because she was her daughter, and had provided Babette with her only grandchild. Now, she had to compete with a woman who was a self-made, high achiever. Sarah was dead set on taking the entire human race to the next level, whether it was ready, or not. She felt envious and terrified of Sarah, all at the same time. The fine line between brilliance and madness was being played out right before her, and she was in too fucked up of a mental state to articulate the ramifications. She now wished she hadn't taken the Percocet.

"Did you know my father on a personal level?" asked Johanna.

Babette tried to picture her father's face, but all she could remember was the guilt and the burden she felt, every time he begged her to take him back. "Yes, I knew him. He didn't think he could raise you on his own, so he helped me adopt you."

Johanna caught herself as her head momentarily bobbed forward. The tiny creases in her forehead deepened and tingled, but she resisted the urge to stroke her face. Yes, she was as high as a kite, and she knew something horrible was unfolding. Too bad her brain was contorted and mangled. All she could think about was the shame she felt for being so weak. She knew they could see it in her eyes, but she still struggled to maintain her composure.

"How many people have you done this to?" asked Sarah, assuming Babette had done the same thing to Johanna's parents.

"You two are my only daughters," said Babette.

Sarah could clearly see that she was lying.

Despite the euphoria and relaxation her pills normally provided, Johanna felt a vague sense of defeat, and wondered what kind of monsters sat before her. She had lived a privileged life, but knew her nannies and the latest sedatives better than she knew her own mother. Dimensions was certainly making more sense to her, as the moments progressed.

An ocean of debris washed over Johanna. She looked in Sarah's eyes and took her hand, envious that she was smart enough to figure out the depth of their mother's betrayal. "So, we're kind of like sisters."

Sarah received her hand with warmth, not knowing what emotion would be revealed by her touch. Johanna felt the hesitancy in her touch, and immediately began to judge her. Sarah's moral compass didn't seem to function any better than their mother's, with this scheme to create a new species out of their children. She needed to do something to stop this insanity, and when her head was clear, she would figure it out. She knew she could stop self-medicating any time she wanted, and now was the time. She would stroll with clarity and face her apathetic addiction demon, if it would help to protect her daughter. After she finished the last six pills in her possession, she would start fresh. Then she noticed the intoxicating aroma of the filet mignon that sat before her. She picked up her knife and watched it cut through the juicy beef like butter, and suddenly, everything that was wrong, was right. The chef had cooked it to a perfect medium rare, and she savored every tender bite as she listened to the flow of life that surrounded her.

Chapter 23

As you slide your bow across my face, I feel the sweet cries of your violin escape my quivering lips. As you slide your bow downward across my heart, I feel the moans of your cello pulsate throughout my mellow veins.

Babette reclined, with her arms extended to the vacant seats on either side in her plush, boxed seats. Her mind and body were relaxed, open and ready to receive. Babette always purchased season tickets for three, but she attended the symphony alone, because it was the only place she felt like she could be herself. There was something about classical music that made her go deep. It created an environment that allowed her to ease her obsession with the terrible revelations of her childhood. Memories that revealed the dichotomy of her parents' personalities; one silently pitted against the other. A dynamic that formed the person she would ultimately become.

She recalled how on Saturday mornings her father would blast Beethoven, motioning his hands high like a conductor, as he danced around the house, preparing to leave for work. Babette never understood why he was always so happy. She hypothesized that it was linked to some gene that passive-aggressively skipped a generation. As soon as her father was out the door, her mother snatched the shades and proceeded to play Dvorak's cello concertos. They would sit together in the big rocking chair, and quietly move to the powerful melodies until they brought her mother to tears. Babette cried, too, sensing it was more than the music her mother was feeling. However, it was only through the trials of adulthood that she understood how music could fillet her mother's emotions raw. Why she insisted that Babette bear witness to it was still a mystery, although it was the only honest memory she had of her mother.

The women of the neighborhood thought her mother had an exquisite manner, with her outspoken hair piled high, and her kitchen always so tight. Every Saturday afternoon, they would line up patiently, waiting for her mother to process their hair. She hated touching other people's hair but, "You've got to make those ends meet," she would always say. Her mother belittled her father at every opportunity. She would jab him with stories of strangers ripping and running in and out of their home, because he wasn't man enough to adequately provide.

Some of those trifling women would show up, time and time again, with filthy hair. Her mother had always told them to wash their hair beforehand, if they didn't want to pay her to do it. Nevertheless, the dirt and oil oozed through the teeth of her hot comb, and the pungent, burning stench would linger. Of course, they apologized, surprised that the filth was so real, but her mother would just watch their lips move, and simmer in silence.

Babette was always the last to get her hair done, and by that time her mother's energy was drained, so her hair never looked as nice as everybody else's. During the week Babette followed her mother's instructions to the letter. Her mother still barked accusations that she wasn't taking proper care of her hair. Ultimately, she would watch in the mirror, stunned, as the brush shattered the strands of her hair like rotten twigs. She couldn't understand why God had cursed her with such bad hair. Her mother hysterically postured over her shoulders, exhaling all the way down to the hands balanced on her hips. Then, without a word, she would leave her side and crawl back into bed until Babette's father returned. Her father worked on a boat, so sometimes he wouldn't return for several days.

She was only ten and just beginning to tune in to the sensations of injustice; she just hadn't figured out what to call it. Babette hated her mother on those days, when she was left to fend for her own emotional stability. In retrospect and as a physician, Babette realized that her mother's severe depression was only a symptom of the psychopathology that teemed below the surface. Her father tried to smooth the effects of her mother's eventual suicide with love, but it never seemed to fill the void.

The symphony was her escape. It was live and always different, because she had an ear for the delicate nuances. Tonight's performance had been exceptionally moving. When the final overtures closed, Babette made her way to the streets, feeling a dangerously new sense of vulnerability. She clutched at her fox shawl, trembling, as she exited the majestic symphony hall and merged with the bustle of the streets. She preferred to walk around the corner, rather than stand in a mile-long queue, waiting for a taxi. The crisp evening air challenged her choice to wear a clingy, golden evening gown, sealed only with an extravagant diamond choker. The further she got from the theater crowd, the more she realized how elegantly she was dressed, and the attention she drew was undeniable. She was sixty-two, but she was still stunning enough to stop traffic, and you would have to beat her ass if you tried to tell her otherwise!

"Excuse me, Ma'am; you need a taxi?"

Babette turned, and almost lost her balance, when she came face to face with the six-foot five inch dark mass that towered before her.

"Why, yes," she smiled awkwardly, and then quickly regained her composure, as she was not one to hide from a man's gaze.

"Right this way, Ma'am."

Babette enjoyed the reverberating rasp of his voice as she followed him to his taxi, then he politely opened the door. The taxi didn't look like a taxi from the outside, but it had all the taxi gadgets on the inside. Yet another foreigner avoiding taxes, she thought to herself.

"So, what's your name, pretty lady?"

"Jones," she said, as she pretended to blush and dipped her head into the vehicle. She typed her neighbor's address into the taxi's GPS, instead of scanning her ID, because she never entered private information into public computers.

He smiled in the mirror. "So, it's me and Mrs. Jones?"

Babette glared indignantly, thinking if only she had a quarter for every time she heard that tired line. "That's Dr. Jones. Take Tremont Street through the South End," she instructed.

As usual, Tremont Street was very busy, with crowds of people moving from their favorite restaurants to their favorite watering holes. The South End was charming, but it had lost its edge. Sometimes, if a city is too safe, the things that once made it great become sanitized during its journey to tony. He turned on the radio, bringing her back. She relaxed, catching his eye and warm smile in the rearview mirror. "So, what's your name?" she asked.

"I'm Maurice, but my friends call me Boogaloo. What are you doing out alone tonight?"

"I was just enjoying a little quality time at the symphony."

"Alone? That sounds depressing."

"One emotion is just as valid as the next," said Babette.

"You need a little jazz in your soul."

"Cha Cha, I've forgotten more about jazz than you will ever know."

"Well, it must not have been too impressive, if you've already forgotten it, and it's Boogaloo." He smiled.

Babette settled back, intrigued, thinking only a man reeking of masculinity could get away with being such a blatant idiot. As they drove down Tremont Street, it was difficult to pinpoint when it happened, but the element of the neighborhood changed. The people were no longer finding their favorite watering holes, but were more like, loitering outside of them.

"You're my last fare tonight, and Mofo's is right up the street. Let's stop for a night-cap."

"That seems wildly inappropriate, Boogaloo," said Babette sarcastically; baffled that he would suggest taking her to such a God-awful hole in the wall.

He smiled in the mirror, and carefully swept his tongue across his bottom lip. Then he pulled into a parking space and turned, smiling from ear to ear, showing a gold molar behind an otherwise benign set of teeth. "There's no way I'm giving up this parking space."

Babette sighed and crossed her legs, "I haven't been here in ages. I guess we could stop for one drink." As he helped her out of the taxi, Babette threw her shawl around her shoulders, and swore to herself that she was going to behave like a lady tonight.

The thuggish security guard boldly made eye contact, and nodded as they approached the door. Upon entering Mofo's, she felt mockingly decadent, as if all eyes were on her. Maurice seemed to know everyone there, like an operator taking advantage of a naïve cougar. Except this wasn't her first time at the rodeo, but she intended to ride him, just the same. No doubt she knew he wanted money; still, she wanted to see how long he would pretend before the night turned into the inevitable business transaction.

The cave-like club was intimately packed to standing room only. She had forgotten the diversity of culture and age that this place drew. It reminded her of a European gem, charming and unpretentious. There was a trio jamming on the stage at the far end of the room. The alto saxophone player played with such desperation, that one contemplated what his life would have been like, without his music. Would he be held up in a clock tower, spraying a crowded courtyard with hot lead, or would he be a conservative family man, not to suggest that the two were mutually exclusive. Either way, no one who played with such emotion could ever fit a one-dimensional profile.

Next to him was the delicately polished double bass that steadied the road, standing taller, and with more confidence than the guy plucking the length of its spine. Finally, there was the drummer, who jerked and twitched more than the sounds coming from his instrument.

Somehow, he still managed to set the pace. Some of the crowd head bobbed, surrendering to involuntary movements of enthusiasm for the art being crafted before them. Others just shook to acknowledge the vague rush that builds inside, when the music was done just right.

"Hey Boogaloo, where's the download at?" said a splashy girl, slinking behind them in a black leather dress.

Maurice smiled and waved, as he continued to push through the crowd to the bar. Babette eyeballed the girl, noting that she must have been half her age and her body was perfectly proportioned with pure youth.

Babette followed him to the bar, where the dim lights brutally outlined his profile. Maurice was one ugly dude, Babette thought to herself. She hadn't been able to place his accent, but his face reminded her of a purebred boxer. She speculated that his raw animal magnetism, and that obscene lump that swayed in his pants, hypnotized women into revealing their worst secrets. Babette's secret was that she self-loathed; in fact, she detested her existence. She had spent thousands of dollars, soul surfing from one therapist to the next, only to learn that the root of her hate was not from within. Instead, she was within it, and it had been slowing digesting her for decades.

She allowed him to order wine for the two of them, though she rarely drank. He allowed her to open her purse to pay, before he reached for his wallet. She slid her hand down the small of his back, and pushed his wallet back into his pocket. Then her hand lingered at his waist for a moment. The dance had begun.

He smiled down, locking into her gaze as he gave her the drink. “What was your name?”

“Dr. Jones.”

“Time is money, Dr. Jones.”

“Yes, and money is power,” said Babette, as she slowly sipped her wine.

He licked his lips and smiled, as he pressed his lower body against her hip, so she could feel his heat. “You’ll know power when we’re done.”

She had a buzz before she knew what was happening. She felt like she was on autopilot, so she excused herself to go to the bathroom and freshen up. As she pushed her way through the crowd, she had to resist the urge to leave the club, settling to just continue to the bathroom and collect herself.

She locked the door behind her, feeling her breath quicken, as the perspiration rose to the surface of her skin. She became startled when she heard someone move in the stall, and suddenly felt claustrophobic, thinking there was barely enough standing room for her. Then, out popped an older black woman with wide moist lips, a couple of missing teeth on the sides, and finger waved hair. Both of her ear lobes were split, like someone had ripped the earrings out of her ears, and then let them heal without treatment. She's lucky she doesn't have keloids, Babette thought to herself. Her shawl had begun to itch. They made eye contact, and the minute she caught her dead gaze, she knew she was in trouble. Not the bodily harm kind of trouble, but the post-surgical sponge count is off, kind of trouble.

"Babbs, is that you?" The woman's deep voice was seasoned from years of cigarettes and cognac.

Babette hadn't allowed anyone to call her that in years. She was sure she didn't know this beat up, old woman. She searched her remote memories, but couldn't come up with anything. "Sorry, you must have mistaken me for someone else," said Babette.

"I don't think so. If you remove that fancy necklace, I'm sure I'll be able to see your roots," sneered the old woman.

Babette wasn't sure what she meant by this, so she just stared, obsessed with the smooth contours of her deformed earlobes.

"I'm Maxine; we ran together back in public school. We were thick as thieves until your mother died. Then you got sadiddy, with your nose twisted like something foul was in your way. I remember you."

"I'm sorry, but that was a difficult time for me." Babette could smell the liquor on her breath and the fact that the woman hadn't washed her hands, did not escape her.

"Uh-huh, isn't that when you need your friends the most?" She pointed her finger at Babette and got close to her face. "Don't you try fronting with me. I know exactly who you are, and I know how you do!" Then she left the bathroom.

Babette's nerves were unsettled. She honestly didn't remember her, and she certainly didn't know what she could have done, to evoke such hostility from so long ago. Babette locked the bathroom door and dabbed water on her eyes, careful not to smudge her makeup. The music echoed against her eardrums, but the sound had begun to feel more distant. Then she caught a glimpse of herself in the mirror, and the shameful old thing appeared, making her nauseous. She had become a voyeur to an aspect of herself she would rather not encounter. Her thoughts began to drift back to her mother, as the beads of sweat formed on her forehead.

After her mother's death, Babette's faith in the human race diminished. Her mourning for her mother turned into the mourning of a narcissistic hoax. To her delight and then her horror, her hair began to grow and it grew to be long, beautiful and luscious. From that moment on, Babette insisted that reality was only what she knew to exist. She felt as if life was merely an inconsequential void between inception and death. It was within her despair, and her reality of nothingness, that she found her integrity.

Now, here she stood, in the tiny bathroom of this old jazz club, with the paint sliding from its sweaty walls. When she made her exit, there was a line of women, waiting to enter. It seemed to take forever for her to find her way back to the bar, where she found the girl in the leather dress, wiggling next to Boogaloo. They smiled, and waved her over for a fresh drink.

She heard a voice that sounded like Billie Holiday, start to sing one of her favorite songs, “You Don't Know What Love Is.” Babette turned, and watched the woman from the bathroom, as she took the stage and transformed into the persona of an urban artist, with hood etiquette and grace. Her voice was beautiful, and Babette instantly remembered who Maxine was. In high school, she had witnessed Maxine’s boyfriend assaulting her, but Babette never showed up to give a supporting statement to the authorities. Tonight, the light, that life seemed to have extinguished from her eyes, had reappeared on the stage. Maxine watched Babette from the stage, as she sang about a restless love, lost in purgatory.

“Why is she still here?” asked Babette, as she redirected her attention to the girl in the black dress.

“That’s my girl, she’s just hanging out. She’s cool,” said Boogaloo.

“Is she splitting the taxi fare with me?”

“No. You’re the only one riding tonight.” Boogaloo laughed.

“Then get rid of her,” she whispered as she slapped a couple of twenty dollar bills on the bar. “I know of a better place we can go. I’ll meet you out front.”

The girl watched her leave. She smiled, never taking her eyes off the diamond choker secured around Babette's neck.

She waited outside, by the taxi, in the chilly evening air, but she didn't have to wait for long. Boogaloo was on his way to play his role in her never-ending insanity.

People say you go crazy, but that's not what really happens. It's more like your mind just turns its back on you. Then you're left wondering if you'll ever get back to the place that you once thought was the worst it could be. That night, Babette tossed and turned in her sleep, until she finally awoke, desperately gasping for air. Her last fuzzy memories of life involved touching the bloody, sucking wound that stretched horizontally across her throat, and finally noticing that her beautiful diamond choker was gone!

At 9:30 a.m. on Sunday morning, Sarah's cell phone rang. "Calm down, what are you talking about?" asked Sarah.

"Sarah, I've been arrested. They think I murdered Babette!"

Chapter 24

The five senses of sight, sound, smell, taste and touch make our worlds more delightfully complex and real. It's been said that when you lose one of these senses, the others become heightened, to compensate for the loss. So, what happens if you lose your sense of self when stripped of your freedom; when the five senses are intact, but your experience of the world is filtered through the intent to punish and reform? It has been said that a heightened compensatory process happens here, as well. Vivian contemplated what her existence would become as she was fingerprinted, booked and hauled into jail, speaking in tongues between each event.

Humbled and with love was the only way to receive God's wonderful blessings, so Vivian didn't pray out of fear. She knew she would walk in peace until she rose to the sacred altar of the Lord. However, deep inside she had been shaken to the core, and she was sure the saints would all be called home on this day. It was now that the Devil would try to have his way with her. Her hatred and bitter attitude would have to change, or her soul would be lost to the trials that awaited her in jail. This wasn't her first dance with the Devil; she had prepared her entire life for such an event. However, Vivian secretly wanted the evil, against which she so desperately prayed, to devour Roree, because she knew he had something to do with this.

"I didn't do this, so I'm not gonna worry, because I know the Lord is in the blessing business," said Vivian, as she peered through the Plexiglas barrier at her daughter.

"I know, I'll get to the bottom of this," said Sarah.

She sucked her teeth. "You can start by checking your husband. You know, you were right, he's nothing like your father."

"Mother, why would Roree want to hurt Babette?"

Vivian had no proof that Roree was involved in Babette's death. She wasn't even sure that Roree was directly connected to the girl in the coma; it was all speculation. It just seemed convenient that suddenly, all of his worries were gone, with her behind bars. Above it all, it warmed her heart to hear Sarah refer to her as mother. "Now, don't get me wrong," said Vivian. "I can't say that I'm sorry she's gone, but I certainly didn't have anything to do with it. We're all God's children, and only He has the right to extinguish another person's life."

"Well, considering your current situation, I wouldn't repeat that warm sentiment to anyone else."

Sarah looked at her poor mother's face, stripped of makeup and dignity, wondering if she was telling the truth. How could she be so ruthless as to have taken Babette's life, for something she did over forty years ago? Vivian's thin, gray hair was combed back into a bun, making her look old, and therefore, innocent. She hadn't seen her without her wig in years. She found it hard to believe that this woman was capable of murder. Of course, in the past few months, she had learned many things that she would consider uncharacteristic, as related to the woman who claimed to be her mother. Sarah searched her own feelings, wondering if she was not capable of the same. After all, every human being had a limit. She left her mother with a mixture of emotions, and a powerful, vague ache.

It seemed that all of the bad drivers were out this afternoon, as she made her way home. The experience of driving hadn't been the same, since she totaled her car seven months ago. She drove more defensively than before, although not even the most strategic driving would have prevented her guardrail collision.

---Home at Last---

Sarah entered her home charged with anticipation, moving as quickly as her legs would permit, up to the bedroom. The room was dark, but she could see that everything was in its proper place. She thought about what awaited her mother in prison if she was found guilty. Sarah replayed the details she got from the attorneys, over and over again in her head. They told her the prosecution had DNA evidence, and that they intended to prove she was a premeditating, spiteful murderer. They also brought up the restraining order that Babette took out against Vivian when she feared for her life, so many years ago. But when she heard that they had collected the DNA from a sapphire and diamond earring, her heart sank. She thought about her pent-up resentment toward Vivian, actually lowering herself to her husband's level. It was there that she dared to empathize with him, and began to think the unthinkable. "Had Roree been hiding it all along?" she thought to herself.

She anxiously fell to her knees and checked Roree's bottom dresser drawer, only to find a pile of underwear, but no cellophane bag. She riffled through the drawer to no avail, and then racked her brain in search of another logical explanation. Christmas had come and gone, and she certainly had never received any jewelry, but she dared not think it was Vivian's earring that glimmered from within that little bag. Finally, having regained her thoughts, she looked up, and was startled by Roree, who had silently darkened the doorway.

"So, how did it go?" asked Roree, as he eased into the room.

"I think she's in shock," said Sarah. She assessed the intensity of his demeanor, and rose to her feet.

"I guess she's just gonna have to pinch her nose and drink the dirty water," said Roree coldly. He glanced between Sarah and the open dresser behind her, before moving close enough to smell the perfumed sweat that leaked from her pores.

"How can you say that? You should see the horrible cage she's in. She thinks you had something to do with this?"

Sarah knew that Roree was ambitious, and she was prepared to support him at any cost, but what if supporting him meant she had to make a shrewd sacrifice? She backed away and searched his face, only to find him shrink under her gaze, which infuriated her. She lunged forward and snatched for his throat. She was alarmed at the pleasure she took when her palm crushed against his Adam's apple, but still, she focused and firmed up her grip.

Roree's eyes popped, caught off guard. Their relationship had been about a lot of things, but it had never been about violence. Sarah was small, and he could bounce her across the room with minimal effort if he lost his cool; if he chose to take pleasure from her pain. Then, his dilated pupils flooded with adrenalin, and the real struggle from within began. The bumping of his heart rose, as the sweaty rage formed on his brow. He choked and instinctively grabbed her wrist, while tucking his chin downward, to interrupt her grip. His muscles tightened like pistons, overheated with fever. Roree's clutched, angry fist was destined to collide with her beautiful, anguished face. His entire body shuddered, but then suddenly froze.

"Mother," yelled Paulis from down the hallway. "Are you up here?"

Sarah looked at Roree's fist and put her fingertip to her lips, shushing him, but she continued to press against his windpipe. The sweat from his neck had covered the palm of her hand. He stared regretfully, thinking about what she had become because of his actions.

Paulis walked into the room and flipped on the lights. He was perplexed by the sight of his mother's hand, awkwardly parked on his father's neck. The two of them breathed heavily, locked in an intense stare. "You two look like you're up to something." He blushed, knowing he had interrupted an intimate moment.

"How's Grandma doing?" asked Paulis.

Sarah lovingly caressed Roree's neck, his fist relaxed at his side. "She looks bad, but she's hanging in there. She sends you her love," said Sarah. Her bicep began to quiver as she held his neck.

"Did you call Terry to see how she's holding up?" asked Roree, while kneading Sarah's shoulder.

"She hasn't returned any of my calls. I don't think she wants to talk to me," said Paulis.

"Paulis, it's been three weeks. Go see her!" said Roree.

Paulis left them and went off to his room, frustrated. He had called Terry earlier that afternoon, and she continued to ignore him, as she had done for weeks.

They were alone again, and Sarah's anger was free to return, but now, with the lights on, her perspective had changed. Though Sarah's instinct was to continue her assault on his throat, she knew that if she pushed too far, she would regret it. "So, I guess I know about all your dirty little secrets now?" asked Sarah.

"Don't play stupid with me!" he exclaimed, anger etched throughout his voice. He felt violated, because she knew he wouldn't raise his hand to her. "You've always known my dirty secrets, our secrets. You've just chosen not to acknowledge them, until you were done reaping the benefits."

Maybe he was right, she thought to herself. She had known of his secrets, and her decisions of action or inaction were equally indictable, depending on the level of consciousness she chose to entertain. Vivian's predicament had certainly made her examine and prioritize the components of her life. But now, she couldn't move forward, because Roree had forced her to choose sides. An aspect of her life was about to die, one way or another. So, what would it be? Would she choose her young family with its unknown challenges, still seeking a stable footing, or would it be the family she lost decades ago?

The Blunts had no grandchildren, and they knew that as soon as the download of the vaccine was successful, the children would become sterile to the rest of the world. However, when coupled with each other, they would create the first generation of genetically corrected post-humans. A new and superior species, poised to achieve beyond anything a mere human could foresee. They would be born with all of the knowledge their parents had acquired and downloaded throughout their lives. Their exponential capacity to learn, love, create and destroy would be boundless, as the generations continued to unfold.

A tear rolled down her cheek, and her head locked in a subtle tremor as she slowly dragged her nails across Roree's throat. She wearily put her heavy head on his chest, before collapsing into his arms. Then she clutched his shoulders in desperation, as a stale stench hung between them, and the bile began to dance at the back of her throat, celebrating the Pontius Pilate she would become.

She was going to miss her mother, but she was about to give birth to the future, and her child would lead the way. It was bigger than her guilt, bigger than her love for her mother, and bigger than her love for God. Where Paulis had once been a timid child, quivering at the thought of life, he would be transformed. Now, the world would bear him and the new species he would spawn.

Roree held her tightly, sensing the unrelenting burden that was upon her shoulders. They breathed in sync and he smiled, though his thoughts were obsessively drawn back to his computer, because he could think of nothing else. Work would be his salvation, as soon as Sarah's evolution was complete, and she could walk, carrying her new emotions.

This moment was inevitable, he thought to himself. His pawn had advanced diagonally, so murder was the only conclusion. Boogaloo was the professional he contracted to eliminate Babette. He was instructed to leave no trace, other than the diamond and sapphire earring. Boogaloo was paid handsomely, and would do just as he was told, because if he got caught, he knew the trail would end with his life.

Now, Roree was a step closer to his legacy, and earning his relevant place in history. Sarah had learned of his actions against her mothers, and he knew she would drag their secret to the grave. But unlike him, the shame would feed upon her like a parasitic fiend, until her soul was hollowed. Her love for him would feel as numb as her limbs. Every time she gazed upon him, her eyes would reflect a guilt-riddled torch. When they made love, her clenching nails would remind him of the sacrifices she endured, as their heat rose, catalyzing their fate.

Chapter 25

---Terry's Space---

Paulis was afraid of rejection, such as that which was demonstrated by the silence of unreturned phone calls. They crossed paths at school, but Terry hadn't engaged him in conversation, and had barely acknowledged his presence. All he wanted was to be there in case she needed a shoulder to cry on. He figured it's what he would have wanted, under similar circumstances. He arrived at Terry's house that night, unannounced. Johanna answered the door, surprised and delighted, but she looked exhausted, as if she hadn't slept in several days. She gave him a suffocating, defeated hug and invited him inside.

"I was so sorry to hear about your mother."

"Paulis, where have you been; I was worried about you."

"I got the impression she needed a little space," said Paulis.

"Don't be silly, you're always welcome here, no matter what happens. How's your mother doing?"

"She's fine, considering." He knew Johanna was just trying to be polite and hadn't heard his reply, and why would she? He wasn't about to explain Sarah's anguish over Vivian's legal matters, while Johanna's mother had been brutally murdered. He thought it was funny how there was only room for the person with the worst situation to openly feel. Everybody else had to suppress, until they were in an environment where their situation trumped, and their emotions could be acknowledged. He imagined what it must be like to live amongst people who were in constant chaos; where it was never your turn to feel.

She led him down the long, white corridor to the den. "Make yourself at home," said Johanna, before leaving him alone, while she went to find Terry.

The den was illuminated by an aged steel chandelier, formed by a bushel of 50 exposed teardrop lights that burst across the room. This was the only room he had ever seen in Terry's house, other than the bathroom. There were big sofas made of top grain leather, and tall, oak slider cabinets with decorative art pieces, gathered from around the world by her father. Backlit family portraits were hung and placed throughout the room. The rugged gentleman smiling in the photos was Terry's father, although Paulis had never met him. Johanna was always captured as happy and bright, standing next to her husband in the photos. The excited, energetic woman staged in the photos only served to mock, in contrast to the woman who greeted him at the door. In fact, the contradiction was downright stunning.

All of the photos of Terry were professionally done at school or in studios, except for the one of the little girl sitting on Babette's lap, with afro puffs and a Cheshire cat smile. They studied in this room, had snacks in this room, and stole quiet kisses in this room, but the rest of the house was an absolute mystery. The maid brought in a tray of chocolate dipped almond biscotti and milk, placing them on the antique steamer trunk coffee table. Paulis sat in the leather recliner, his favorite seat. He imagined it must have been her father's favorite seat as well, considering the room seemed to be arranged around it. He always got a thrill as his back sank into the leather, while he simultaneously stroked the cold, riveted stainless steel sides, trying to discriminate between the two sensations.

Paulis stood in shock when Terry first entered the room. She wasn't wearing her head guard, and all of her beautiful hair had been cut off. He saw her mournful eyes, and was reminded of a wounded puppy. It had been three weeks since Babette's funeral. "I was so sorry to hear about your grandmother," said Paulis. His apprehension and fear quickly dissipated, when he realized her emotions had nothing to do with him. The hurt in her eyes was so distant and firm that no one could reach it to make it better, to make it less lonely, less helpless. Terry wasn't trying to be reached.

"My grandmother told me I didn't know anything about life, and I needed to respect history." She laughed, and looked him in the eyes, wiping a tear from her cheek with the back of her hand. "Thank you for the flowers."

"My pleasure," said Paulis.

“You know, she was always there for me. Why would your grandmother do this?”

“I don’t believe she did.”

“Why would anyone do such a thing? Why would she do it?”

Paulis felt her anger and confusion. He also felt that this was not a rhetorical question. “I don’t believe she did it! They arrested her because our grandmothers had a history.”

“What history? Paulis, they found her DNA all over the scene!”

“You must hate me, if you really think she did this. My grandmother is fierce, but she wouldn’t harm a fly. Besides, I heard some things about your grandmother hurting people. She could have had enemies. Things are rarely as they appear. If I’ve learned anything in life, I know that to be true.”

“Well, my grandmother is gone.”

Paulis hugged her and sighed. “In a sense, so is mine.”

There was no hate in Terry’s hug. His thoughts returned to his parents back at the house. Something didn’t seem right. They were at odds, but clearly maintaining the calculated family unit, for his benefit.

Paulis had watched his father suppress intense anger for as long as he could remember. He probably thought that not acting on his anger meant it didn't exist, but you could see it shining out of him. He may not have claimed it, but that only gave it the power to take on a life of its own, where anything was possible. Strangely enough, it had been his mother who seemed to be hostile, and controlling the situation.

"Maybe we can help figure out who really killed your grandmother. Then we can be together, and put all of this negativity behind us. My family always sticks together. Maybe I can show you what that means. Someday, I can show you what it means to be part of the Blunt family."

Terry grabbed his hand. "Follow me. I have something I've wanted to show you."

They went through the kitchen, which was littered with matching stainless steel appliances and shiny doodads, on the way out of the back door. It was a quiet, peaceful night. You could see the full moon, hovering like a filtered sun. A gentle breeze dusted his cheek. He was in love like never before, and it felt like life had just shared its most cherished secret. She led him around the pool area, and over to what appeared to be a guest house.

When they entered the building, they were immediately overwhelmed by the smell of electricity. As they moved further into the room, he noticed that not only was it dark, but all of the windows were blacked out. Terry disabled the alarm system, and all of a sudden the lights popped on. He did a quick panoramic survey of the room, noting the ceramic tiled floors and soapstone countertops along the beige walls. "Wow, where did you get all of this?" asked Paulis, gawking at what looked like two mini MRI machines. There were two boxy leather and chrome chaise lounges sitting face to face, each connected to three monitors projecting from above. The mini MRIs were connected to the head cushions of the chairs, like high-tech hair dryers.

"This is an older model my dad used to sell, but my grandmother helped me put this whole thing together. The software that runs the system was my idea," Terry gushed with pride. "We combined parts from several machines, and modified them so that they're not strong enough to give off any measurable radiation. As a result, they can no longer produce brain images. However, they can transmit thoughts through here." She pointed to the round tablets, suspended like steering wheels above each seat, as she circled the machine.

"We call it GABA Rap. Do you want to try it?"

"What does it do?"

"It's like a thought-provoking video game."

"What exactly does that mean?"

"Remember when you said, you wished you could touch your thoughts to mine? Well, be careful what you wish for. It has levels of difficulty similar to what you would have with a video game. The first level is mostly manual. You choose a thought in your mind, and then press enter. The thought will reoccur as a preview in your head, and unless you press delete within five seconds, the thought will be transmitted to the person hooked up in the other chair. The intermediate level randomly transmits past thoughts. It's usually something you've pondered recently. The advanced level allows you to freely transmit your thoughts in real time, without an opportunity to edit or filter. I suggest we start at the advanced level. It would be like ripping off a Band-Aid." She laughed with anticipation.

Paulis chuckled awkwardly. "How do you know if it translates into accurate thoughts?"

"I'll let you be the judge of that, when we're done."

"What if I'm thinking about something I don't want you to know?"

"Then I guess you're not ready to share as much as you thought. My grandmother used to say that there's always a level of truth that's being hidden." Terry pointed to the machine. "This removes the filter. She also cautioned that if you shared the advanced level with someone who had severe mental illness, it could negatively affect you."

Terry watched him inquisitively, still feeling alienated from his inner world, yet drawn to his quiet power. "Paulis, have you seriously thought about what's happening to us? Our parents are planning our mating schedules as if they were part of a tradition; like we're from some third world nation."

"There's nothing wrong with a little tradition, and if you recall, the difference is that we chose each other." He smiled warmly.

"We don't know what sex is like, or what our children will be like. What if all of these changes being made to our bodies produce deformed or retarded children? What if God already got the right balance, when he created us?" Then she closed her eyes as if in pain. "Am I going to be enough for you?"

"What is that supposed to mean?"

"What if I'm gay?" She exhaled deeply.

"Why, did you make a decision about something?" His breaths had become shallow and rapid.

"There's no decision to be made. I just don't want to lie or rationalize to myself or you. I know that having the gene doesn't automatically make me gay. By the same token, I don't believe that being hyper-focused on the issue, and having our peers react as they do, would cause me to be gay, either." Terry lingered on Paulis's word, "decision," realizing that she was in the unique position to ponder the age-old debate. Unfortunately, the answer was blurred by her despair, and only the utmost periphery of her despair would ever be acknowledged as real, because any action she took would be deemed as a choice.

"I guess on some level, even before the genetic testing, I've always questioned my sexuality."

"So, I guess the real question is, am I going to be enough for you?" asked Paulis. "You think maybe you're bi?" Paulis smiled, allowing his words a moment to grasp at any false hope available, and then he lowered his head. "I guess there's no test for that."

"I hadn't even thought about that." She felt heartache as she watched the disappointment in his face. "Paulis, it's not an issue until it's an issue. I love you and that's never going to change. Besides, we're not sexually active yet, so what difference does it make today?"

"You and I both know it's not that simple. We've been intimate friends and we've confided in each other. I hope that hasn't changed." He glanced at the MRI contraption, quietly thinking about his grandmother's lecture on denial. Terry followed his eyes.

"Has it changed?" he asked.

"Nothing's changed. Oh, so, now you want to try it?"

Paulis's eyes drifted over the length of the GABA Rap, mesmerized with curiosity. She took his head guard off and placed it in a cabinet against the far wall. They sat down on the two opposite chaise lounges, toe to toe, and booted up the big machine. They settled their heads back on the head rests, and pulled the black domes over their heads. Paulis observed that the monitor to the left would display Terry's brain activity, and the one to the right would have his. The monitor in the middle displayed gaming options, by level of difficulty. They both agreed to try the intermediate level, the level that shared random past thoughts. They simultaneously touched the screen selection to activate the program.

"Now, keep your eyes closed until it's done," said Terry.

First, there was darkness, and only the quiet, rhythmic hum of the machine could be heard as it transmitted a warm sensation to the head and neck. The seats eased back as the lumbar support first widened and then slowly moved in, stopping just lateral to either side of his spine. A wave of gentle vibrations followed. Paulis was relaxed, and was caught off guard when an image appeared. The image was that of Terry, seated on the sofa with her back to Babette, who combed and stroked her hair. Occasionally, Babette pulled her head back and said something directly to her face. All he could hear Terry say was, "yes" and "I will," over and over again.

The image Terry saw was that of an older woman sprawled out on a crisp, white sheet, stroking her naked body. Paulis was seated at a computer, almost paralyzed, as he watched her. The woman appeared to be upset with Paulis, but he never responded to a word she said. All she could hear was his heavy, steady breathing.

When the session ended, they both pushed the black domes up off of their heads, and rose from the reclined seats. Paulis squeezed his eyes and shook his head. “So, what did you see?” he asked.

She described what she saw, and Paulis panicked, wondering if she saw more than she claimed. Maybe she was testing him, to see if he would tell the truth.

“You must have seen the woman that used to come to me in my dreams.”

Terry smiled. “I didn’t realize I would be able to see your dreams, but I was hoping that’s what I was seeing. Why was she so upset?”

“Who knows, it was just a dream,” said Paulis, without making eye contact.

She took his hand. “So I guess I’m not the woman you’ve been dreaming of?” asked Terry sarcastically.

Paulis blushed and rolled his eyes. He hadn’t dreamed of the naked woman since taking the translational psychiatrist’s additional download.

“How about you?” asked Terry. “Tell me what you saw.”

He watched Terry’s face, as he described the images he saw of her with Babette. “What was she saying to you?” asked Paulis.

"That could have happened on any number of nights. What you saw was my grandmother trying to encourage me to rise above it all, like she did. She told me that love was for the weak, but if I had to love, then I should do it like a greedy bitch. She told me to expect the worst from people and not to apologize for being who I am. She also said that if I wanted something, I needed to claim it and then never, ever give up!"

Paulis stared at her intently, with silent, cautious eyes. "Did you try the advanced GABA Rap with her?"

"Paulis, the old girl was a little out there, but she wasn't mentally ill, if that's what you're implying. Personally, I just think she liked playing with my hair."

"So, what are we gonna tell our parents?" asked Paulis.

"There's nothing to tell, it's not an issue until it's an issue. Besides, our parents work for us." Terry smiled and gave him a kiss on the lips.

Paulis received her lips, and decided not to regret it. He stroked the back of her head and gazed into her eyes. Terry looked older and sterner, like someone had threatened to push her too hard. "So, why did you cut your beautiful hair?"

"My grandmother would never let me cut it. I've always felt like it was covering up my nice bone structure," she said, studying his face.

Paulis pondered her words in disbelief as he observed how strong her features had become, now that they were no longer hidden by her long hair. However, he knew this butch haircut was designed to uncover more than just her bone structure. “They’re not stupid, you know?” said Paulis.

“The smarter they make us, the more stupid they’ll become. Anyway, people tend to see exactly what they want to see,” she said, smiling.

Paulis laughed out loud, but he knew she was serious, and though he didn’t want to admit it, he also knew she was correct.

They were young, and they had the energy to change the world, but the world was rooted in very old traditions. They would first have to disrupt that which the world had known as truth, before insinuating their newness onto its stripped palate. Then, after their position was understood, they would settle back, look the world in the eye, and observe as they adapted.

---THE END---

---*About the Author*---

Steven Wooden is a Michigan State University and St. George's University alumnus. He grew up in Detroit, then lived and traveled abroad before finally settling in New England. Steve currently lives in Boston and works at the University of Massachusetts Medical School. He is also working on his second novel, *The Fall of the Offspring*; the sequel to *Dimensions*.

29098287R00165

Made in the USA
Middletown, DE
08 February 2016